TAXED TO DEATH

For Maya

TAXED TO DEATH

By

DEBRA PURDY KONG

*To my esteemed
writing colleague.
Enjoy!
Debra Purdy Kong*

GYPSY MOON PRESS
Port Moody, British Columbia
1995

Canadian Cataloguing in Publication Data

Kong, Debra Purdy, 1955-
    Taxed to death

ISBN 0-9699211-0-1

    I. Title.

PS8571.0693T39 1995   C813'.54   C95-900529-3
PR9199.3.K633T39 1995

Printed in Canada by Benwell-Atkins Limited
2nd Printing, 1997

Gypsy Moon Press
3313 Henry Street
Port Moody, British Columbia
CANADA
V3H 2K4

AUTHOR'S NOTES

This book has been a tremendous learning experience over the past thirteen years. Friends, family members and acquaintances have offered valuable input along the way, and I truly appreciate their help. I'd like to thank Winnifred Assmann for her copy editing and proofreading skills. Thank you, also, to David Lester for designing a fabulous cover, and to the Coquitlam Writers' Group for their astute advice regarding the book's production.

A few souls, such as Valerie and Tom Rix, deserve special thanks for supporting my efforts with this project from beginning to end. Tom's expertise with computers saved me from a technological nightmare. I'd like to thank my husband for cooking all those meals while I wrote on weekends. Many thanks to my mother, Vivian Purdy, for her support and the countless hours of baby-sitting. Finally, a big thank you to Elida and Alexander for being such great kids. Without their cooperation, I wouldn't be a writer.

This is a work of fiction. All characters are imaginary and bear no resemblance to any person living or dead. Every event, including those involving Revenue Canada, are entirely the product of the author's imagination. The interior layout of Revenue Canada's West Pender Street branch has been fictionalized, and although I've placed my imagined Special Investigations Division at this branch, the real-life Special Investigations Unit is located elsewhere.

Some settings, such as the Skylark Hotel and the gambling casino on an island off the coast of Sechelt, are imaginary. Also, Silby & Morrow, Chartered Accountants, Ice Craft Jewellers and Lions Imports do not exist.

This novel is dedicated to my best friend, husband and favourite accountant: Bark Kong.

ONE

The intruder's search through Andy Gowan's living room was quick, methodical and neat. He wore gloves to avoid prints. He was careful to return objects to their rightful places. In the bedroom, he scanned the files in a black metal filing cabinet, until he heard the lock on the apartment's front door click open. The intruder hurried across the room to a closet crammed with clothes, shoes, and stacks of boxes. Turning off his flashlight, he hid behind the boxes and waited.

Entering the living room, Andy switched on a lamp and a soft rock music station on the stereo, while Alex Bellamy opened his audit briefcase and scattered half a dozen files on the floor.

"This is great!" He sat among the files with his legs outstretched. "I'm surrounded by fraud. It's all over your carpet, Andy."

Andy massaged his aching left shoulder. "I wish you hadn't dropped your end of the bookcase last weekend."

"I know. I'm sorry. After three months in that town-house, I'm still tripping over the threshold twice a week. I don't understand it."

Andy understood. The guy couldn't survive two days at a campsite without hurting himself, but accidents had never dampened his enthusiasm for the outdoors. Last winter he'd wanted to try helicopter skiing but Andy hadn't found the courage to go with him, and Alex was too smart to try it alone.

"Did you see the look on Sam Roche's face when we showed up in his office?" Alex opened the nearest file and peered over his glasses at Andy. "There's nothing like a surprise audit by Revenue Canada to suck the blood from a man's face. Course, under the circumstances, I can understand why he wasn't told we were coming."

"I'm sure that Alfred Lin, as the owner of Ice Craft Jewellers, would have been warned. Whether he wanted his staff to know was another matter." Andy loosened his tie. "Want a shot of Drambuie?"

"Since when do you keep liqueurs in the apartment?"

"Since my job promotion."

Alex followed him into the kitchen. "Why do you think someone in Special Investigations took us off the audit?"

"Who knows?" Andy poured Drambuie into juice glasses.

"Strange that it happened right after we verified that the gems Roche bought on behalf of Ice Craft weren't part of Ice Craft's inventory."

"S.I. never explains its behaviour to junior auditors, Alex."

Alex ran his fingers through his tangled, golden-brown hair. "Especially if someone wants to cover something up."

Andy handed him a glass. "You're not serious?"

"Think about it." He sipped the thick, sweet liqueur and nearly choked. He'd never been big on sugary alcohol, but every so often he wanted to see if his taste had changed.

"While Alfred was out of the country, Roche decided to buy a hundred and fifty thousand bucks worth of precious stones. He also made sure that Lions Imports, who sold the stones to him, was paid immediately."

"So?"

"So what if seller and buyer shared the gems and money with someone in Special Investigations? Which would be why an audit was suddenly stopped by their division without explanation."

Andy swirled the liqueur in his glass. "You're jumping to conclusions."

"Maybe, but haven't you wondered how S.I. found out about the audit so fast?"

"I assumed our supervisor told someone about it. Maybe S.I. was already investigating Ice Craft or Lions and didn't appreciate our help." Andy paused. "Or maybe the bookkeeper who worked for Roche contacted their division as well as ours. This investigation started because of her allegations about Roche's rather unusual activities as Ice Craft's controller."

"Roche could have called someone in S.I. about us. Remember when we told him who we were, and he said he thought there'd been an arrangement?"

"He could have been talking about the timing of our arrival."

"Then why didn't he say so when I asked him what he meant?"

"Maybe it was the way you asked. You do get a little abrasive when taxpayers aren't as cooperative as you'd like. Besides, don't you think pulling off a fraud like that would be a little stupid? If Roche was ripping off Ice Craft, surely he'd have covered his tracks better."

"Maybe the guy was too desperate for money to care at that point, which makes me wonder how Roche spends his pay cheques." His eyes sparkled. "It could be fun to find out."

The brighter Alex's eyes shone the more worried Andy became. He remembered Alex at age fifteen, often annoying his teachers with endless questions. He didn't do it on purpose, and the questions were intelligent, but he'd had a five-year-old's curiosity and persistence. Worse still, he could never turn down challenges. In twelfth grade, he ran the school newspaper, played basketball, served on the student body, and still aced exams. When his grandmother died a month before his graduation, he nearly had a nervous breakdown.

"Whether Sam's a crook or just incompetent," Andy said, "he'll have to care now. I imagine Alfred Lin isn't happy about the way Roche handled things while he was away."

Alex gazed at the lemon-yellow cupboard doors he'd helped Andy paint last year. He had hoped to talk Andy out of splashing bright colours on his living room walls, but interior design wasn't his friend's strong suit.

"I've heard about conflicts between staff members in Special Investigations," Alex said. "Missing files and accusations of improper behaviour, whatever that means."

Andy had heard similar rumours. This enigmatic division of Revenue Canada investigated taxpayers suspected of lying on their tax returns. He'd once thought about joining the division, but the work was tedious and often unrewarding. In complex cases, hundreds of thousands of bits of paper were analyzed to provide enough evidence for a conviction, and months of work were sometimes wasted because of crafty lawyers and pathetically light fines.

"I can't believe our people would be involved in a cover-up, Alex."

"Our people?" He grinned at Andy.

"You think that the possibility of Revenue Canada's involvement in some sort of fraud conspiracy is funny?"

"I think it's bizarre and possibly humorous, but so what? People cheat on their employers all the time. So who in S.I. ordered us off the audit?"

"I don't know." Andy swept strands of thick red hair out of his eyes. "I have a couple of friends in that division. They might know if anyone's taken an interest in Ice Craft or Lions Imports."

"Good." Alex followed him into the living room. "I've been doing some checking on my own. . . ."

"Is that why you disappeared this afternoon?"

"I went to see Tristan Wells. He's the articling student I told you about. Works at Silby & Morrow."

Andy slumped into a lumpy, green plaid armchair. "Ice Craft's accounting firm?"

"Exactly. It seems we weren't the only ones the company's bookkeeper contacted about Roche's activities." He stepped over a file. "She also called Silby & Morrow's senior partner, Les Silby, which is why Tristan's appearance at Ice Craft was no coincidence."

Andy sighed. He watched his friend restlessly survey the room and wished he'd sit down and relax. "Did you tell Tristan about the missing gems?"

Alex was the world's biggest gossip. He was always the first in the office to learn who was pregnant, or divorcing, or changing jobs. Andy watched him stroll towards the bedroom.

"I told Tris enough to convince him I'm right about a fraud cover-up that involves someone in S.I."

Andy gripped his glass. "Are you out of your mind?"

"Tristan thinks he can back my theory."

"How?"

"I'm not sure. He wants to check a couple of things before he says more."

In front of the bedroom door, he lifted his arms above his head to stretch. Suddenly he stopped and turned around.

"What's the matter?" Andy placed his glass on the floor and untied his shoe laces.

"Nothing. Just thought I heard something." He poked his head inside the room and flipped on the light switch. "Oh, God!"

"What?"

"Your room's a mess! Don't you ever clean it?"

"The last Sunday of every month," Andy replied as he pulled his slippers out from under the chair, "if I remember."

Alex turned the light off and returned to the files on the

floor. He reached for one of the Lions Imports folders.

Andy watched him browse through the documents. "When I was at Tony Barker's office, looking at Roche's purchase from Lions Imports' perspective, nothing in the records suggested anything unusual about the transaction."

"Which is why I think he helped Roche cheat Ice Craft for a share of the profits. You told me Barker keeps tight control of his business. If he was innocent he would've questioned the size of Roche's purchases."

"How do you know he didn't?"

"Because he would have had to call Alfred Lin, and Lin's already confirmed that nobody called him about the purchase. His secretary had a phone number where he could have been reached. Besides, Alfred's never bought that many precious stones over a two-month period before, and he's never let anyone buy gems on his behalf."

Andy thumbed through the TV listings. *Casablanca* was on soon and he never missed a chance to see the movie. "You shouldn't have discussed the case with outsiders, Alex."

"Les Silby's glad I did."

Long brown eyes quickly narrowed. "You didn't tell him, too!"

"He looked interested when I told him my suspicion about a connection between Roche, Barker and Special Investigations. Even if he doesn't believe me, Les knows something's wrong, and since both Ice Craft and Lions Imports are his clients he wants to find out what's going on."

"I still don't see why he'd discuss the situation with you."

Alex gazed at him. "Did you know that every copy of Lions' latest financial statements and corporate tax returns are missing from both our offices? You told me Barker couldn't find his copy of the statements either."

Andy nodded. "And?"

"Whole sets of statements wouldn't disappear from three

offices without a reason." His eyes shone with excitement. "I think Les has doubts about Barker's honesty, which is why he didn't throw me out of his office when I talked to him this afternoon, and why he's agreed to let me help him find out what the deal is between Roche and Barker."

Andy's face turned mauve. "You're a Revenue Canada auditor! You can't go around making special deals with public chartered accountants."

"Too late."

"I think you should return all the files to our supervisor and let somebody more experienced handle this."

"You worried about me, Andy?"

"Considering your past with hostile professors and employers, I should be."

Alex tapped his thigh in time to a Billy Joel tune on the stereo. "If we proved that people used their positions to take part in a fraud, we'd make a name for ourselves pretty damn fast."

"The opportunities and promotions will come, Alex." Andy massaged his sore shoulder. "You've only been with Revenue Canada six months, and if you pry too much you could lose your job."

"I turned twenty-six four weeks ago which means that, according to Bellamy tradition and expectation, I should have launched a promising career by now."

"And a junior auditor's job isn't good enough when one's brothers and sisters are running hotels and building financial empires?"

Alex glanced at the orange carpet and the bare beige wall. "It's not exactly what I or my parents had in mind."

"None of your siblings started out six thousand miles from home like you did."

When Alex was seventeen, his parents moved to Montreal, leaving him with his ailing grandmother. It was Alex's choice. When she died, he stayed in Vancouver. Again his choice. He rarely talked about the separation from his family. He'd never complained about his parents, though, and as far as Andy knew, he'd never quarreled with them.

"So, Andy, will you help me find out who's behind the fraud?"

He watched Alex pace around the room, his eyes flitting from the low, makeshift bookshelves to the TV that sat on a card table. "I can't afford to lose my job."

He nodded. "I know, but now that you're in a more senior position, maybe you can find out who's been running things in S.I. over the last couple of weeks."

Andy hesitated. "I'll talk to my friends."

"Thanks. Meanwhile, Les Silby's secretary will be giving me some information on Lions Imports so I can learn more about the company's financial history. The lady's name is Jillian and I hear she's gorgeous."

Andy rested his elbows on his knees. He wanted to slip out of his suit and into his bathrobe before *Casablanca* started.

"There are less risky ways to get ahead in the world, Alex."

Alex fiddled with a gold cross around his neck. "This is about stopping one scam in a fraud epidemic that's already costing taxpayers billions. It drives me nuts to think that someone who's paid to catch the cheaters is cashing in on their profits."

Andy checked his watch. "*Casablanca's* on in two minutes. You can watch it here if you want, provided we don't talk about work."

Alex removed his glasses and held them up to the light. "I should be going. Thanks for buying dinner."

"Thanks for helping me celebrate my promotion."

"It was fun. Does your dad still need help fixing his cottage this weekend?"

"Yeah, I'll let you know when we're leaving. Thanks, Alex."

"Okay, and don't worry about the audit. I know what

I'm doing, sort of."

"Where have I heard that before?"

Andy saw Alex out, then slid the brass chain across the door. He strolled down the hall, stopping to turn off the kitchen light. Paul Simon sang softly from the stereo. Andy eased his suit jacket off his sore shoulder. He thought about tossing it on the bed but this was his best jacket.

He switched on the bedroom light, took one step forward, and stopped. A man wearing a ski mask stood before him with a flashlight raised to shoulder level.

As Andy started to back up, the flashlight struck his jaw. He slumped forward, dropping the jacket. He tried to straighten up, tried to lift his arms to fight back, but the flashlight was too quick. It hit him on the side of his head. Another blow left him unconscious.

The intruder lifted him onto the bed and pressed Andy's fingers around a brand new razor blade. He then bent his right hand back by the fingertips, exposing his wrist. With his hand firmly on the blade, the man swiftly sliced Andy's wrist open. He cut the other wrist and left the blade by his left hand. Quickly, he stuffed his blood-smeared gloves into a plastic bag brought for this purpose.

Removing his mask, the intruder stepped away from the body. He'd have to keep Alex from talking to Jillian Scott, and from finding the Lions Imports financial statements.

As he turned the bedroom light out, the intruder shone his flashlight on Andy. His red hair looked orange next to the dark red blood. The kid was grotesque on the bed, torn and helpless. He smiled at the thought of doing the same to Alex Bellamy, then hurried out of the apartment, confident of reaching Alex before the young man spoke to another living soul.

TWO

The late show was on when Jillian Scott's telephone rang. She listened, then touched the receiver, but didn't pick it up: not this time. Last year's crank caller had taught her not to leap with every ring. It was better to sit here quietly than to satisfy some creep's need for attention. She'd already answered the phone twice tonight, and he'd pretended not to be there, just as he had last night and the night before, so why not step out of the game?

Jillian rocked back and forth and waited . . . four rings, five, six. The noise hurt, like a tick burrowing into sunburned skin. Seven. Why didn't he hang up? Eight. All she wanted to do was watch this woman's story on TV. Nine.

Last summer, the calls had come between midnight and four a.m., and that guy had used his voice. The jerk had been vulgar, smug, and easily amused. She'd slept little during those weeks, until she got an unlisted phone number. How had this creep gotten her number?

Last night, somebody rang her apartment buzzer at one-thirty in the morning. After searching the place, the police told Jillian that her "prankster" was gone, and since she lived on the eleventh floor, the threat of real physical harm was remote.

Jillian hadn't told them about the crazy man who, three months ago, found his way to the roof and began jumping down onto balconies to reach his ex-girlfriend's apartment:

the apartment that was now Jillian's. It was fortunate he'd crashed onto the wrong balcony, just as it was fortunate this caller was mute. Good luck had always approached Jillian this way, although lately she'd been wondering if her luck would run out. Twelve.

She grabbed the receiver and brought it back down so hard a wobbly table leg fell on the floor. The table started to topple, and she caught the phone just before it slid off. She quickly placed the phone on the floor. Her hands shook as she screwed the leg back into worn grooves. She couldn't let him control her life. She focused on fixing her table: a cute, antique walnut piece bought on sale. All of the antiques in her apartment were bargains; this was the only one with loose legs, though.

As Jillian carefully placed the phone on the table, she thought about taking the receiver off the hook, but this was Wednesday, Dad's bowling night. If he stayed out too late Mom would call and want to talk until his return. Anyway, why shouldn't the line stay connected? This mute little creep wasn't a threat; hardly worth mentioning to friends or co-workers, not that many would care. A second crank caller in eight months would seem too strange to take seriously.

Jillian stared at the phone. She'd never slammed the receiver before. If her caller got mad and changed his approach, if this freak was crazy. . . . For a moment she thought about asking a couple of friends over; on the other hand, why bother people when she hadn't actually been threatened? Maybe the caller was just a lonely twelve-year-old kid with nothing better to do. Then again. . . .

A plate of soda crackers covered with hardened strips of cheddar cheese sat on the coffee table. She reached for a cracker, changed her mind, and picked up the water glass next to two sleeping pills. She carried the half-full glass to the kitchen and turned on the tap for cooler, fresher water.

By the time she returned to the living room, the movie's heroine had gotten married, given birth to triplets, and been voted woman of the year for good works done for appreciative charities. The heroine wasn't a secretary, Jillian noticed. She'd never heard of a secretary who'd been voted woman of the year. Not that it couldn't happen. It just wasn't likely to happen to her.

She picked up the file she'd brought home from the office, stared at the first page without actually reading the words, then put it down again.

An issue of *New Woman* magazine slid off the coffee table as Jillian reached for her personal goals list. She read: "Take trip to England for antique tour; start jogging; enroll in self-defence course."

She sighed, then wandered onto her balcony to gaze at the lights of Vancouver's North Shore. On the mountains, the lights of the ski lifts dangled like diamond bracelets on black velvet. Further along, she tried to picture the silent impenetrable mountain peaks called the Lions, now blackened into obscurity by the darkness. In daylight, the peaks were plainly visible, encased in massive snow tombs. When the sun appeared, even those who were blind and emotionally crippled sensed their presence, proud and challenging, brimming with mountaintop secrets. Jillian looked for the Lions. She knew they were there, though she couldn't see them, and she knew an enemy was out there, but she couldn't hear him. She shivered in her nightgown.

The last evening of March was cold and dry. An icy wind swooped past her. Stepping inside, she wished she hadn't skipped tonight's walk. It wasn't necessary to stay home to prove her fearlessness to some jerk with a phone fetish. Jillian knew what could happen to people who stayed inside too long. She'd watched her mother grow petrified of the world as her agoraphobia took root, then deepened to the point where even stepping into the backyard made her scream.

She'd begged Jillian not to move out: had warned her about peepers, muggers, and rapists. The more she talked, the smaller the house became, until Jillian felt as if she'd been buried alive in the same box with her parents. To keep similar fears from surfacing in herself, she walked every evening after supper. It wasn't always easy.

She stood in the middle of the living room, hugging herself and sneezing repeatedly. Spring had barely arrived and tree pollen was already on the attack. She reached for the box of Kleenex tissues on the coffee table and wondered if it was safe to take a Seldane tablet with sleeping pills. Suddenly, someone screamed.

Jillian turned to the TV and saw the movie heroine in an ambulance while real sirens blared under her balcony. Stepping outside, she looked for smoke or signs of an accident. She looked at the apartments beside her, then cautiously peered at the balcony above.

There was no sign of a leaping maniac. Jillian locked the glass door. Then she unlocked it and locked it again. Pressing her nose against the glass, she stared outside. No one was there. No one was waiting to swoop down and maul, mug, or rape her.

Quickly, she dialled her mom's phone number. "Hi, it's me. How're you doing?"

She relaxed at the sound of her mother's voice, until Mom said, "So, Jillian, what are you up to?"

"I'm trying to psych myself up to finish some work for Les."

"When will you learn to say no to that man?"

"Soon."

"You've sounded awfully unhappy with your job lately."

Jillian hesitated. "It's just that after six years with Silby & Morrow, Chartered Accountants, things have gone from boring to demoralizing."

As her mother rambled on about job opportunities for experienced secretaries, Jillian remembered when Les Silby first promoted her from switchboard operator to secretary four years ago. She was surprised and flattered by his confidence in her potential. She worked hard to learn the job and to know his clients. Once, she had been reproached by the eldest partner, Martin Sloane, for knowing too much. To appease him, she played dumb until Martin forgot she knew anything important at all. Now, she was the one who was forgetting things.

She'd begun to misplace Les's correspondence and various office supplies at an alarming rate. Files had been found in the women's room or next to the postage machine. Any day now she expected to find herself sitting on a street corner, typing on an invisible word processor and asking strangers when they'd be back from lunch.

"Listen, I've got to go, dear; your dad just came home."

Gently, Jillian replaced the receiver, then wrote "find new career" on her personal goals list. She stared at Les's file. Overtime had become a regular part of her life. Computers hadn't eased her workload, and coffee still had to be carried to the boss's office. Still, she could live with the job a little longer, if Les weren't so miserable these days. He was the real reason for her insomnia.

His worst moods occurred when he lost a client or was about to fire an employee. With the Ice Craft situation, Jillian suspected it was both; yet, whatever he'd held against her lately seemed to remain lodged in his throat until she was afraid he'd spit it at her. Her memory lapses were probably annoying the hell out of him. She'd let him down; maybe she was the one who'd be fired.

The other day, he'd glared at her during his meeting with Alfred Lin, though Alfred was the one who'd been giving him a rough time. While Jillian served coffee Alfred had questioned Les about Tony Barker's relationship with Jerry Margolin. She'd seen the dismay in Les's eyes as he quietly asked what Jerry, as his tax partner, had to do with Ice Craft's missing inventory. Alfred had waited until she left the room before he responded.

Jillian gazed at the file's contents. Les wanted a

breakdown of services the firm had provided for Ice Craft over the last six months. Their controller should have handled it, but Les didn't want the guy asking awkward questions. If she got up early tomorrow she could probably finish the work by eight o'clock. Tomorrow was Thursday, April 1, April Fools' Day; two more days until the weekend, then two wonderful days of sleeping in.

In the kitchen, she cut a small slice of chocolate cheesecake she'd made from a favourite recipe, and brought it to the living room. As she savoured the taste of chocolatey cream cheese and sour cream, Jillian gazed at a photograph on the wall opposite her: a picture of herself and three small children. One boy's head was wrapped in bandages, the second boy was leaning on crutches, and the little girl was bald. The photograph was taken at Children's Hospital last summer, at a birthday party for the boy on crutches. Jillian had volunteered there twice a week then and had organized parties all the time.

She eased herself onto the living room floor and tried to remember who she'd given her phone number to over the past month. Slowly she raised her right leg ninety degrees in the air. The caller could be someone she knew, an acquaintance playing a practical joke.

Jillian pointed her foot, then gently flexed it, and pointed it once more before lowering her leg. She repeated the movement with her left leg, then lifted both legs together and flapped her feet back and forth.

She missed her ballet days: the sweaty exhilaration as each class progressed from simple warm-ups to grand jetés across the floor. After her mother got sick, she couldn't drive Jillian to lessons. Her father worked during the day, and as neither parent wanted their twelve-year-old daughter riding buses, she'd had to quit. She'd never stopped exercising, though. A little stretch before bed was a good relaxant: probably better than sleeping pills.

Lowering her legs, Jillian's toes caught the edge of her

sewing basket and spilled three small puppets onto the carpet. Quickly, she gathered the puppets together. It was almost Easter and she still had three tiny outfits to finish sewing before they'd be ready for her girlfriend, Donna, and Donna's kids. She missed spending time with her friend, but since January there'd always been Les's work to think of, Les's needs, Les's wants. She closed her eyes and listened to the TV heroine sob in her wheelchair. Fatigue swept over her body as she crawled to the TV and shut it off.

Brushing her teeth perked her up enough to reach for her copy of *Pride and Prejudice*. In bed, she read half a page before her eyes began to close once more. Jillian placed the book on her night stand and snuggled under her quilt. At last, sleep came easily, until the telephone rang.

THREE

L es Silby scowled when Jillian limped into the boardroom, and tugged on her grey wool dress to hide a hole in her pantyhose. A large canvas bag thumped against her hip as she passed an agenda out to Silby & Morrow's five partners.

"What happened to you?" he asked.

"Just a slight mishap on the bus."

The zipper of some guy's gym bag had latched onto her hosiery like a leech onto soft porous skin. When Jillian pulled herself free, she fell down the exit steps and landed on her left hip. She could practically feel a glowing purple bruise spread over her skin.

Hobbling past the sofa, she winced at the smell of old Scotch. Although the tax partner, Jerry Margolin, had offered to clean up the drink his client had spilled last Thursday night, Les had ordered Jillian to clean the room, then had badgered her until every paper and sticky coaster had been removed. On her way to the door, she handed the last copy of the agenda to Les.

"Don't go yet, please," he said.

Turning around, Jillian was abruptly nudged in the backside.

"Morning, Jillian; your lovely butt's in the way." Tristan Wells brushed past her and placed some files on the low square table in front of Les. "Here's all the Ice Craft files."

"Have a seat, Mr. Wells." Les opened the first file. "Has anyone found the Lions Imports statements?"

Sam Roche's fraudulent transactions with an unknown individual at Lions Imports made Les nervous about the disappearance of the company's corporate statements and income tax returns. He'd begun to worry about the accuracy of the numbers in those documents.

"Isobel had the working paper files last," Craig McBride remarked.

Jillian watched Craig tap a cigarette package on his chubby thigh. Every year, his thighs grew fatter, his face rounder, his head balder. He was beginning to resemble a large beach ball with skin.

Craig had accepted John Morrow's employment offer on the condition that he'd be considered for partnership a year after joining the firm. Three months after Craig was made a partner, John died. About that time, Craig stopped putting in long hours, but nobody, except Martin Sloane, complained because he brought a lot of clients to the firm.

"You're mistaken." Isobel Cameron looked at Jerry. "Didn't I give the file to you a few days ago?"

"Yes," he said, frowning at his agenda, "but I thought I gave it back. Martin, did I give you the file?"

"I don't have it!" Martin glowered at him through smudged and greasy glasses. Dozens of tiny white flecks spotted each lens. "May we please get started? I have another meeting in an hour. Jillian, we need coffee in here."

"Hold it." Les swung his arm in front of Jillian. "I have an errand for her first." He reached for a pen and paper.

"Isobel," Martin said, "can you get the coffee? Perhaps the blessed statements will show up in the kitchen."

Isobel gazed at Martin with glossy brown eyes. Although Isobel had been with the firm for nearly twenty years and was a highly skilled auditing partner, Jillian often saw Martin treat her like a waitress. He wouldn't think of asking a male partner to serve coffee, because that would be a joke, and his specialty was insult.

When Isobel left the room, Craig lit a cigarette. "She probably can't find the damn file and just won't admit it."

"She's made a bloody mess of Lions Imports," said Martin, returning Les's frown. "The woman can't handle Tony Barker and doesn't understand his business. Tristan will tell you. He's had to come to me for answers."

"That was about one of your files, Mr. Sloane."

Martin's eyes bulged and his mouth puckered poisonously. "It was not!"

"Sure it was."

"Thank you, Tristan," Les said as he quickly glanced at the files. "It looks like I have everything I need, so you can leave now."

"Don't you want my report on the Ice Craft situation?"

The room became silent. Jillian watched the partners glance from Tristan to Les. "I can manage, Mr. Wells, thank you."

Isobel brushed past Tristan as she carried two mugs of coffee into the room. She handed Les a mug, then sipped from the second one. "My apologies, gentlemen, but there was only enough coffee for two." She ignored Martin's furious gaze. Craig smirked while Jerry kept his eyes on the agenda.

While Les slowly wrote a list on the notepad, Jillian noticed how the partners had automatically separated both sectional sofas so each person had his or her own space. Craig usually pushed his chair close to Isobel because there was only one ashtray in the room and they both smoked.

Les always occupied John Morrow's large wing-chair. This room had been John's office that Les turned into an informal boardroom because everyone used to meet here anyway, and Les didn't want people gathering in his own office.

"Here's the places to search for the Lions statements." Les handed Jillian the note paper.

Jillian raised an eyebrow. In addition to the filing room, he'd listed his partners' offices. "I'll start now." She hurried out of the room.

"Since the subject of Ice Craft has been raised," Les said as he thumbed through a file, "I'd like to review the situation."

His plan had been to end the meeting with this topic, which was why he'd had Jillian distribute agendas at the last moment; however, as tempers were already flaring it was better to get this over with before someone stormed out of the room.

"Are we facing a lawsuit?" Martin asked.

Les studied his anxious expression. "We're not Ice Craft's auditors. All we've ever done for Alfred's company is prepare financial statements and tax returns. I've reviewed the statements, though, and the numbers are correct. All generally accepted accounting principles have been adhered to."

"Yes, but since we prepared audited statements for Lions Imports we're damn well trapped in the middle if Tony Barker's company is liable for anything."

After talking with Alex Bellamy, Les was convinced of Barker's role in the fraud. He hadn't told his partners about his conversation with Alex. He didn't want to alarm them without real evidence.

Martin yelled, "What will happen when people find out we prepare financial statements for criminals?" He clasped his hands together. His fingertips pressed the backs of his hands until the purple veins throbbed. He'd spent most of his career worrying about lawsuits brought by angry clients or shareholders. Martin had heard of hundred million dollar claims against public accounting firms in the United States. The Ice Craft situation was as close as his fears had come to reality, and all he could hope for was that any error or indiscretion wasn't his fault.

"What does Tony Barker say about all this?" Isobel

brushed Craig's cigarette ash off her black and coral dress. He'd propped the ashtray between their chairs.

"Nothing he'd want us to hear, I bet." Craig watched Jerry jot something down.

"As far as Mr. Barker's concerned, his company made legitimate sales to a client," Les replied and sipped his coffee.

"I heard Sam Roche is hiding the gems he bought," Isobel said.

Les stared at her.

"There've been rumours," she added.

Les glanced at each of his partners. "Roche accused an unnamed party at Lions of keeping the stones plus twenty-five percent of the cash Ice Craft paid for them."

"Then the jerk's claiming he's innocent of fraud?" Craig asked.

Les held his coffee cup with both hands. "Not exactly. He's alluded to certain mistakes on his part, but he's also made it clear that others are involved. The problem is he's not prepared to name names yet."

"God Almighty!" Martin wiped his face with a crumpled cotton handkerchief. "What kind of controller behaves like that?"

"Looks like Roche has dynamite strapped to Barker's balls." Craig leaned back in his chair and spread his legs further apart. The inside seam at the top of his thigh had begun to split open.

"Tony's not necessarily involved in this," Jerry said quickly. "He probably didn't even know what was happening. He has other businesses to run, and since his vice-president's illness he's been too busy to keep tabs on everything."

Les stared at his tax partner. Tony Barker was a close friend of Jerry's and one of his most important clients. Les had never approved of their friendship. It wasn't right for a client to entangle himself in his accountant's private life to the point where they spent almost every weekend together.

"Mr. Barker's involvement hasn't been proven," Les

replied, "yet only two other people at Lions Imports have access to the stones. One is the vice-president who suffered a heart attack seven weeks ago. The other is the controller whose activities are apparently under investigation."

"Who's investigating?" Craig blew smoke in Isobel's direction. "The cops or Revenue Canada?"

"For the moment, Revenue Canada, though I'm not sure where it's going. The auditors were called away from Ice Craft before they'd finished the job."

Isobel threw him a puzzled glance. "Why?"

"I don't know. It's a complicated situation."

The incident was one of a dozen complications invading his firm recently. Compounding the usual problems were increased workloads and frequent conflicts between partners. Every partner felt the strain but Les wasn't sure if any of them understood what was happening. No one spoke of the tension and any personality clashes were blamed on the latest recession, income tax season, or minor annoyances.

"So, people, how will we protect ourselves and our clients without demolishing everyone's reputation?" Les asked. "By the way, Mr. Barker called yesterday to complain that his accounting matters, aside from personal tax issues," he glanced at Jerry, "have been grossly mishandled. He said different C.A.s and partners have asked him the same questions every month and I'd like to know why."

He watched Martin glare at Craig, Craig stare at Isobel, and Isobel smile at both of them.

"Craig, I gave you the files to look after," Les said irritably. "What happened?"

"I didn't have time for Lions."

"Did you sign the auditor's report in the statements?"

Craig studied his senior partner's harsh expression. "No."

"Then who did?"

No one answered. Suspicion about the numbers on those audited statements nibbled at Les. If the numbers were wrong, then how wrong were they?

Looking at Craig, Martin opened his mouth to say something, then stopped.

"It seems Mr. Barker's accusations are justified." Les stared at his partners. "Is there anyone who hasn't handled Lions Imports yet, or should I give the file clerk a shot at it? Surely she couldn't do worse than the talent in this room." The telephone rang. Les answered it then turned to Jerry. "Your wife's on the phone: some sort of emergency."

Jerry jumped up. "I'll take it in my office."

When he left the room, Craig said, "Mrs. Margolin probably can't decide what colour to paint her toenails." He tapped his lower lip with his finger. "Have you ever noticed that Marlena's partial to red? I'm partial to peach myself." He glanced at Isobel's peach-coloured nails.

"Wives," Martin grumbled, "always phoning and whining and nagging." He checked his watch and stood up. "I have to leave for my client's office."

"We'll cover the other agenda items tomorrow morning," Les stated. "Please be here at eight-thirty sharp."

As Craig started to protest, Les walked out of the boardroom. He stopped at Jillian's desk.

"Any luck finding the Lions statements?"

"I went through the filing room, but they weren't there. Since then I've been busy taking your calls." She stood up to hand him a stack of messages. "It seems a lot of clients want to meet with you to discuss income tax issues."

She glanced at his bloodshot eyes, at the lines on a face almost as grey as the hair creeping over his collar. A recent weight loss made his six-foot, two-inch height appear painfully stretched in a fifty-seven-year-old man.

"You haven't given me your date book yet," she added, "so I'm not sure how many appointments to arrange."

"I'll give it to you later this morning. Meanwhile, keep looking for the statements."

Jillian's left eye began to sting. She rubbed it, then sat

down and retrieved a tiny mirror from her purse. "I finished the Ice Craft work last night and early this morning."

"I'll look at it after you've found the statements." He stepped inside his office and closed the door.

She spotted a loose eyelash just below her iris and gently freed it with her fingertip. While she brushed layers of short dark hair around her face, she rehearsed a carefully prepared speech about reducing her overtime hours. She was summing up her case when the telephone rang.

"Mr. Silby's office."

The line was silent.

"Hello?"

The line was still silent. Deliberately silent. A hot, glowing red ball rolled through Jillian's stomach.

"Hello? Hello!"

She hung up and pushed her chair back from the desk. She thought of telling Les about the anonymous calls but decided it wasn't worth the risk of discovering he was as short on sympathy as he was on patience; not when she was hanging from the top rung of the clerical ladder by her chin. Any minute she could fall, live out her life in a cave where everything was calm, peaceful and silent.

She hurried down the corridor and, in the kitchen, found a freshly brewed pot of coffee. Her hand shook as she filled a mug. To calm herself, she read the latest barrage of Martin Sloane memos to clutter the bulletin board. A warm gush of air suddenly filled her ear and she jumped, spilling coffee on her hand.

"Sorry, my love." Tristan Wells handed her a paper towel.

If there was one person she didn't want to be near today, it was Tristan. He had a way of prying into her life without encouragement or conscience. He propositioned her constantly, ate her jelly beans, and left pictures of naked men on her desk with inscriptions like, 'my brother Joe, the shrimp of the family,' or 'the best is yet to come!' scribbled on torsos. Jillian liked the pictures; she didn't like receiving them from Tristan.

"Shall I kiss your hands better?"

"No."

Dark blue eyes gazed at her from a smooth, red-cheeked complexion that gave Tristan a deceptively wholesome appearance, for Tristan Wells was as wholesome as green bacon on mouldy bread. She wondered if he was her silent caller.

"Do you like my suit?"

Jillian glanced at Tristan's navy pinstriped suit, noting it matched his eyes perfectly. Tristan owned four pairs of coloured contact lenses, which he liked to coordinate with his clothes. Once, in a moment of weakness, he had exposed his own murky, greenish brown eyes. Jillian glanced at his trousers and wondered if the rest of him would be as disappointing.

She tossed the towel in the wastebasket. "Very nice."

"It's my brand new Sedley-Tremblay suit." Tristan pirouetted and flashed a bright red lining. "I named it after two guys involved in a stock swindle. They got caught because Sedley broke a date with his girlfriend to go to bed with his own wife. The girlfriend found out, got pissed off, and told the police about the swindle. So, the guy was screwed because he screwed the one he should have been screwing in the first place."

"You're making this up."

Tristan smiled. "I could make you a pile of money through similar stories."

"I prefer a daily interest savings account." Jillian sipped her coffee and grimaced at a salty pungent aftertaste.

"That's because you've got a bad case of bookkeeper's mentality."

"Which means?"

"It means you need advice but won't take it." He tucked in his shirt. "All clients want to know is how much money they can save and what it will cost to learn how. I could teach any bookkeeper that if she'd listen, but no, pierced ears cause deafness, which is why most rock stars can't sing."

Jillian sipped the coffee. Her silent caller couldn't possibly be Tristan. Tristan wouldn't be able to phone her without saying something stupid.

"Did you know that Les asked me to help Alfred Lin get a bank loan?" he asked.

"What are Alfred's chances?"

"Not great. I'm going to plead insanity with a lot of accounting jargon and a whiz-bang balance sheet and hope the bankers are too dumb to see through the poop. The trouble is, Canadian banks only lend money if you can prove you don't really need it. They won't look past a balance sheet. If this was the States, then the banks would consider a company's future. Down there, an accountant's opinion represents security, knowledge, sincerity—"

"A lot of B.S."

"It's business, Jill. It's also chargeable time, which means our boss gets to send out large invoices so you and I get paid. You should thank me for all the pay cheques I've contributed to on your behalf."

"Now I know why the cheques are so small."

"If you don't like the money then get into tax. That's where the big bucks are." He smacked his hands together. "Income tax specialists control the wealth and power in this country. They help the economy by making sure businessmen keep their profits. Let's face it, taxes are screwing everybody and I say it's time to fuck back."

Jillian stared at him. "That's really profound, Tristan."

"So maybe reality's profound. Personally, I don't give a shit. All I know is that someday I'll be making over two hundred bucks an hour bailing people out of tax jams."

He strolled to the table pushed against the wall and picked up several pink phone slips. "Are these yours? The handwriting looks familiar."

26   Taxed to Death

Jillian gazed at the messages that had disappeared from her desk yesterday. "Yeah." She studied Tristan's face. "Thanks."

"You know," he murmured close to her ear, "I heard that Sam Roche threatened to take a couple of people down with him if he loses his job at Ice Craft."

"That sounds like something Sam would say."

Tristan looked over his shoulder. "Apparently, one of the people he could ruin works here."

"Not you, by any chance," she said, then winced over another mouthful of coffee. "This stuff tastes really weird."

"Oh?" Tristan's mouth twitched as he struggled not to grin.

Jillian peered at her mug until Tristan began to snicker. She looked at him. "What?"

"APRIL FOOLS!" He collapsed with laughter.

Jillian dumped the coffee down the drain. "What did you put in it?"

Since he was laughing too hard to answer, she sniffed the pot, then took a spoon from the drawer. She swirled it around the coffee until a greyish brown clump appeared in the spoon.

"What the hell is that?" Jillian stared at the lump in horror.

"It's just a joke; don't take it personally. You just happened to be the first one here."

"I said, what was in the damn coffee?"

"A few anchovies. I didn't think you'd drink half a cup before noticing," Tristan remarked, then laughed again.

Jillian's throat swelled as a thick anchovy slime coated her tongue. She marched out of the kitchen as Tristan started to apologize. He'd never been good at apology, and she never could stay out of his traps. With most people she could hold her own, but when it came to Tristan she fell out of the boat every time.

At her desk, she popped three jelly beans in her mouth.

She retrieved a financial statement from the hard drive and, reading from the draft pages by her keyboard, typed "the future tax benefit of the additional income tax value of the depreciable assets has not been recognized in the accounts due to uncertainty as to its ultimate realization." Jillian sighed. She'd never understood what that line meant; half of the C.A. students didn't know either.

Silby opened his door and escorted Jerry Margolin out. "Jillian, would you tell Tristan I want to see him?"

"I'll get Tris," Jerry offered. "I need to talk to him anyway."

Jerry was Jillian's favourite partner. He was helpful, polite, and had never made her feel like she'd just crawled out of a cave to experience the privilege of working for a superior being.

"How're you doing, Jillian?" Jerry asked.

"Okay, thanks."

She liked the way his mouth crinkled under his moustache when he smiled, and Jerry smiled a lot. He had good reasons for happiness. Jerry Margolin was a brilliant income tax specialist and head of the tax division at thirty-four years of age. Recently, he'd stopped working evenings to be with his new wife. Jillian missed Jerry's company at night and hoped Marlena appreciated the nice guy she'd married.

"Jillian, can we get together now?" Les re-entered his office.

"Sure."

She reached for the file she'd worked on at home the night before, but it was gone. She searched her desk and the floor, then took everything out of her canvas bag. She wanted to ask Les if he'd taken it, but she'd already asked after so many things this week.

Jillian stepped into Les's office. She glanced at every chair and table top. The file wasn't there. She stared at the room's decor, an act of rebellion from John Morrow's era when Les was desperate to break free of his conservatism. Shortly after John's death two years ago, Les divorced his wife and placed his part of the settlement in here because this was his home and always had been.

"I want to set up a confidential meeting with our lawyers as soon as possible." He thumbed through the stack of work on his desk. "Martin will take over Craig's T1 responsibilities this year and you'll have to show his secretary how to assemble tax returns."

Jillian looked at her boss. Normally, he would have commented on Craig's reaction to the change.

"Also, someone from Revenue Canada, a man named Alex Bellamy, is coming to look at the Lions Imports files for the last three years. I'd like you to pull the files out of storage right away."

"Okay."

"I told Alex to see you and he'll be here soon." Les kept his eyes on his work. "He may ask you a couple of things about Lions. I'd like you to cooperate with him."

It wasn't like Les to release information this way. It wasn't like him to avoid her eyes either.

"Are things okay with Lions?"

"That's what I'm trying to find out."

Jillian gazed at the small lacquered box Alfred Lin had given to Les nearly four years ago. The box was rectangular, six inches long, its lid decorated with small, delicately painted flowers. The buds, coloured violet and plum, lightened into soft, translucent mauve in the open flowers.

"Les, is there anything you don't want this Bellamy guy to know about the company?"

He thought about it for a moment, then shook his head.

"I suppose there isn't much he doesn't already know or won't find out. Now, you said you had some work for me?"

Jillian stood up. "I'll be right back."

"On second thought, maybe you should go to the storage room first."

At her desk, she removed a key from a drawer and tugged on her dress again to cover the hole in her pantyhose. Glancing at the scattered contents of her canvas bag, she picked up a plastic container of chocolate cheesecake. She hurried down the hall, colliding with Tristan as he left Jerry's office.

"So," she stepped back, "what'd you do to Jerry for April Fools' Day, burn his desk?"

"Are you okay? You look tired and a little frazzled."

As Jillian continued down the hall, she said, "Tell me you dumped the coffee pot out before a partner got hold of it."

"I'm touched that you don't want to see me in trouble."

"I just wouldn't want anyone throwing up in the kitchen, because I'd probably have to clean the mess."

Jillian reached the reception desk a second after Jerry. She knew he'd be sympathetic about her anonymous calls. Maybe she'd ask his advice later today. Jillian turned to the receptionist, Connie Sekata: a twenty-five-year-old redhead, part-time karate instructor, and lover of cheesecake. She'd offered to teach Jillian some karate moves. Lately, Jillian had thought about taking her up on the offer.

"I'll be in the storage room, Connie, and here's a sample of my latest cheesecake. I forgot to give it to you when I got in."

"Jillian!" Connie took the container from her. "Thank you."

While Jerry quietly spoke with Tristan, Jillian leaned close to her. "I got a call this morning, a little after nine, but I didn't catch the man's name. Do you know who he was?"

"There haven't been any calls for you." Connie pried the lid off the container. "Les had two or three calls, though; did you get those?"

"Yeah, I did, thanks."

Her stalker must have asked for Les, knowing she'd

screen the call first. Jillian walked to the elevators. How much did this creep know about her?

"Connie, I'm just popping out to the store." Tristan followed Jillian as Craig and Isobel strolled past them.

"Next time I'll bring my burglary tools," Craig murmured.

"Try it and die," Isobel replied.

Jillian stared at them as the elevator doors slid open.

"You didn't offer me any cheesecake," Tristan said. "I'm hurt."

"You don't deserve a piece today. Maybe next time."

"I'd be grateful." He stepped into the elevator after her. "Where are you off to, my sweet?"

"The dungeon."

"Would you like an escort? It's pretty dark down there." His eyebrows twitched and his mouth puckered lustfully.

"I'm not old enough to need a sleazy Boy Scout."

"Have it your way, anchovy breath."

"You're sick, Tristan."

The doors opened and they stepped into the lobby of the building.

"That's why I work at S & M, get it?"

As she marched towards the parking level elevators, she said, "Les is looking for you."

"Yeah, Jerry told me, but I want to get a newspaper before the store runs out. Back in a flash!" He then ran towards the main exit.

Jillian sighed. She missed the original gang of secretaries, C.A.s, and students who joked and shared lunches when the firm was fifteen people strong, and John Morrow was alive. She used to think that expansion was good for the firm, but since it had doubled in size too much had changed.

She'd seen the popularity and influence of employees grow, peak, and fade as office friendships and camaraderie dissolved with the resignation notices. The new staff, people like Tristan and Craig, had altered the atmosphere of the firm to the point where she'd become the outsider, the one who didn't understand what was going on.

The storage room on Parking Level One was long, rectangular, and dusty. Shelves jammed with file folders filled every wall and boxes were stacked high in the middle of the floor. Jillian yawned and left the door open to let fresh air in. She was pulling the Lions files off the shelf when someone tapped her on the shoulder.

"Excuse me."

A man near her own age and height stood behind her. His lower lip was split open and swollen. Two long cuts intersected on his left cheek. Jillian stepped away from him. "I'm sorry," Alex said anxiously. "Did I scare you?"

"A little."

"I was told you'd be here." His smile was crooked, tense. He adjusted his glasses. "My name's Alex Bellamy. I'm with Revenue Canada."

Jillian studied the cuts on his face. "What happened to you?"

"I was attacked three nights ago." He glanced at the doorway. "Les Silby said I could talk to you about Lions Imports. Could I buy you a coffee?"

She looked at his blue jeans and grey sweat shirt. "I thought you guys wore suits."

"I took the morning off. Thought I'd look over the Lions material before I went to the office. I know a place where we could talk without distractions."

The guy seemed nice enough and, despite the cuts, wasn't bad looking. "I guess it'd be okay. Let me get my coat and purse."

"Jillian, there's no time; we've got to talk now." Again, he glanced at the door. "Please come with me."

"I'll only be a couple of minutes." She tried to walk around Alex but he blocked the exit.

Jillian stopped. She thought of the anonymous calls, and

the colour left her face. An intense heat washed over her back and climbed up her neck.

"Oh no."

Alex tried to lead her out of the room. Jillian pulled back.

"No! Take your hands off me!"

"Jillian, we have to talk about Ice Craft and Lions Imports!"

"Oh, God!" She tried to free herself from his grasp. "Somebody, help!"

As he clamped his hand over her mouth, she dropped the files. She threw her weight to one side and started to kick him when he jumped back, releasing her right arm. She punched his face. The cuts on his cheek glistened with beads of blood.

Alex tried to haul her out of the room but Jillian held onto the doorknob with both hands. The door slammed shut. When she wouldn't budge, he grabbed her around her ribs and pulled. The elevators were directly ahead, but both cars were at the lobby level. Soon, the P1 light flashed on. He pulled harder. Jillian held on. Her muscles screamed as she prayed for help. The orange light flickered to P2. This was happening to someone else; she was just watching. She always watched; never participated, ever.

Suddenly the pressure left her ribs. She looked up and stared at the gun pointed at her stomach.

"I'm really sorry. I don't want to do it this way, but you've left me no choice!"

Perspiration surfaced on Jillian's forehead and upper lip. She felt dizzy, segregated from her own body.

"Everything will be fine," he said as the gun trembled in his hand, "if we can just talk some place private."

She had started to shake her head when her eyes slowly closed and she collapsed at his feet.

FOUR

Martin Sloane charged into Les's office. "Leslie, what in God's name is going on? Someone just kidnapped your secretary!" His face was red and blotchy, and he was trying to catch his breath.

Les spun around. "Jerry, I'll call you back." He disconnected the speaker phone.

Martin waited for Les to absorb the shock. The situation called for immediate action, a show of leadership, but his partner just sat there, as if unable to grasp the seriousness of his announcement. Martin resented the way he'd been left, since John Morrow's death, to fight staff members tempted to cheat the firm for personal gain. The battles were affecting his health. Cancer and weak hearts had destroyed his father's family; diabetes, senility and blindness had plagued his mother's pathetic bunch for years.

"Leslie!"

"Martin," Les said as he put his pen down, "what are you talking about?"

"I saw a man dump her in a car and drive off. She looked unconscious, for God's sake!" His lips tightened into a frantic purple knot.

"When was this?"

"Five minutes ago." Martin wrung his hands together. "I was halfway to my client's office when I realized I'd forgotten a document. I'd just pulled into my parking spot when I saw him carry her out!"

Les stared at Martin's greasy glasses, at the bulging eyes about to burst through them. "What did the man look like?"

"Young. Brown hair and glasses."

Alex Bellamy, Les thought. What the hell was he up to?

"It doesn't make sense, Leslie. Jillian isn't worth anything, is she?"

"She doesn't come from a wealthy family," he answered coldly, "if that's what you mean." Les scanned the notes he'd written while speaking with Jerry.

Martin didn't understand his partner's reaction. Why didn't he look worried or at least a little shaken?

"Leslie," Martin said as perspiration turned his white bangs into mottled yellow spikes, "we've got to call the police!"

"Look; someone from Revenue Canada was meeting her this morning. Maybe they discovered they knew one another and were just having some fun."

"Neither of them looked like they were having much fun."

He reached for the phone but Les clamped his hand over the receiver. "There's no point in panicking until we know what happened, and if the police need to be called, then it's my responsibility."

"All right, fine," he answered pettishly. His displeasure with Les's leadership was a permanent vexation he no longer wished to hide. "If she isn't back by noon then you'd better call a partners' meeting."

"I'll think about it."

Les looked over his mail while Martin wondered how they could come up with one or two hundred thousand dollars on short notice. The problem would have to be dealt with quickly and efficiently. As Martin considered the options, he began to see an advantage to this nightmare, a means of obtaining overdue recognition. It was a matter of getting a head start: forming a plan while the others still groped with their whys and wherefores.

When he left the room Les tossed his mail to one side. Alex had been anxious and abrupt on the phone this morning. Jillian was mentioned briefly with respect to the Lions files, but that was all. She knew a lot about the Ice Craft situation, however, plus other confidential matters that might interest Alex. Les tried to rub away the headache that had begun a slow, rhythmic pounding at his temples. Closing his eyes, he suddenly remembered Jerry, and hurried into his office to find Jerry's wife and Tony Barker gazing at him expectantly.

Barker must have been the appointment Jerry was waiting for when Les called him. He wondered whether they'd quietly walked in on Jerry while they were talking on the speaker phone. Les was still annoyed with Barker for spilling Scotch on his boardroom sofa last Thursday night. He'd seen the way Barker had carelessly plunked the bottle down when he'd walked in on his and Jerry's discussion. The clumsy idiot had probably knocked the damn thing over.

"I'm sorry to interrupt," Les muttered, and looked at Jerry, "but I wonder if I could borrow your secretary this morning."

Barker gave him a warm smile. "How are you, Les?"

Marlena stood up. She was wearing the same nauseating perfume she'd worn at her wedding. The aroma, if one could call it that, was horribly sweet and pungent, as if someone had boiled molasses and vanilla with heavily scented flowers. Worse still, the woman seemed compelled to douse herself with the concoction from head to foot. No one could have smelled anything else at that wedding. No one could have forgotten her when she left the room, which, Les suspected, had been her plan.

"We'll have to go soon, darling." She walked around the desk and massaged Jerry's shoulders.

Les said, "One of Jillian's friends has carried her off somewhere."

"I see." Jerry glanced at Barker. "A boyfriend, no doubt."

Barker laughed. "That's what happens when employees fall in love. Marlena hasn't worked a full day since I introduced her to Jerry."

"If you didn't expect so much then you'd be satisfied, wouldn't you?" She winked at him.

Les wondered if Marlena knew about Sam Roche's fraud scheme. As Barker's personal assistant, she'd have access to all sorts of information, including financial records. The woman was also an opportunist who enjoyed material comfort far too much.

"Nice seeing you both again." Les left the room, spotted Martin in the corridor, then turned and headed in the opposite direction.

Martin followed him as far as the reception desk. "Connie, did you see—"

"Yes, I'll tell him," she said to a caller.

"Did someone from—"

"No, he shouldn't be much longer. Yes I will, 'bye now."

"Connie!"

She hung up.

"Did someone from Revenue Canada come to see Jillian or Les this morning?"

"No."

"Are you sure?" He glared at the startled receptionist.

"Yes, I'm sure." She stared at him. "Why?"

"I want the name of every caller Les has today."

"A lot of people phone him, Mr. Sloane."

"When Jillian's away you screen the calls, don't you?"

"She's here, though."

"She is not here!"

"I usually put his calls straight through. Les doesn't mind."

Martin folded his arms. "When Jillian's not here, you're to find out who's calling, that's your job."

A call came in for Martin. He took a pen from his pocket

and handed it to her. "Get me a new refill, will you?"

As he rushed back to his office, Connie murmured, "Go to hell."

She hated the way Martin Sloane stuck his nose in everyone's business. He'd been known to open employees' mail, read their phone messages, and eavesdrop on conversations.

She had no intention of becoming office snitch for Martin's benefit, which was why she wasn't going to tell him about Mr. Faust, the sexy sounding Revenue Canada guy who often called and, while waiting for his party, asked all sorts of questions about Les and the other partners. Only yesterday, Mr. Faust was joking about Martin's meddling nature and how, with a little luck, he could be forced into an early retirement one day.

FIVE

Someone tapped on Kelly Faust's door. Faust swiftly locked the Lions Imports file in his bottom desk drawer, and closed his eyes for just a moment. He then forced himself to smile pleasantly.

"Come in."

His secretary hurried in carrying half-a-dozen Special Investigations file folders and a small cardboard box. "Lunch time, Kelly."

He clasped his hands behind his head. "Aren't you going out?"

"I thought I'd bring you something first."

Inside the box were two enormous chocolate éclairs.

"Thanks for trying to get the staff a new cafeteria."

Faust stared at the éclairs. Nobody had ever bought him éclairs before. Nobody had bought him a present in years.

"I wish it had worked out. The support staff deserve a better room."

Becky was always running errands for him and ensuring that his life ran efficiently. It had taken Faust twenty-five years at Revenue Canada to earn his own secretary, and when this intelligent, energetic woman arrived, life became almost tolerable.

Faust met Becky's gaze and quickly looked away again. His lips felt three times larger than normal: grossly disproportionate to his long narrow face. Although he'd never been overweight, small pockets of flesh hung below his cheek-bones. He removed his glasses and rubbed his eyes. He blinked at the photograph of his father, a foot-high portrait hogging space on his desk. His father had never liked secretaries. He'd come home from Revenue Canada every day, grumbling about their malevolent attitudes. When he was sufficiently irritated, he'd hit his wife and accuse her of similar behaviour. As he put on his glasses, Faust studied his father's face: a slab of pork with eyes.

"I heard your dad worked here for nearly thirty-two years."

Faust looked at Becky.

"Was he the only family you had?"

"Yes." He gazed at the éclairs. "He left me the portrait in his will." He didn't add that the photograph was all his father had left him.

"You must have been very close."

Faust leaned toward the cardboard box and inhaled deeply. The sweet smell of chocolate and cream wafted from pastry that smelled so fresh it was probably still warm.

"Would you like one of these? I couldn't eat two."

"Are you sure?" Becky's hand was already on the larger pastry. "I guess you heard about the kid in Audit who killed himself last night."

Faust picked up his éclair. He was right. It was slightly warm. "I heard a little. What have you heard?"

"That Andy Gowan was a nice guy with a promising future. He had no personal problems that anyone knew about, so why would the kid kill himself?"

"I don't think anyone wants to kill himself." Faust laid his éclair on the napkin Becky provided. "I think a person just reaches a point when he knows he has to."

She stared at Kelly, then slid a file towards him. "The work you did on the Bugliani case was returned. The attached memo says more evidence is needed for court."

Faust studied his manicured fingernails. He couldn't

count the number of times his work, recommendations, and ideas had been rejected by supervisors: people he'd once trained to work well and conscientiously.

Becky handed him a sheet of paper. "This form's about the Easter barbecue. The Social Committee wants to know if you'd prefer wieners, hamburgers, or chicken." She strolled to the door. "The other files you wanted are also there."

"Thanks, Becky." Faust scanned the labels. "I don't see the Talbo file."

"Darius Ridgegold has it."

"How come?"

"I don't know. He took it off my desk yesterday; said he had to borrow it for a couple of minutes and never gave it back."

Faust brushed his hand over thinning hair. "Don't give anyone files without my permission, okay?"

"Sure. I should warn you that Darius also wants the Carlee file."

"Did he say why?"

"No, but then he wouldn't. The guy's so damn secretive."

"He's an important man," Faust said, then smirked. "At least he likes to think so."

He smiled until Becky left the room. For several seconds he stared straight ahead, then slowly pressed the digits of Ridgegold's local.

"Darius? Hi, it's Kelly. I understand you're looking for the Carlee file." He unlocked the bottom drawer. The Carlee file was tucked under the Lions Imports file, and the files of two dozen other fraudulent taxpayers who were indebted to him. "I'm afraid I don't have it, Darius. . . . No, I didn't hear the rumour. What's happened?"

Faust relocked the drawer as he listened to his colleague.

"I didn't think a promotion announcement would be made until next month." He sat upright. "Why did they choose that guy? He hasn't been here long enough to qualify, and who told you others will be laid off?" Faust asked quietly. "Who's going? . . . Well, I guess I'll find out soon enough."

As he hung up, Faust wrapped his hand around the drawer's key and squeezed hard. This was the sixth promotion to pass him by, a ritual he'd learned to expect, if not accept. Angered and confused by the rejections after his third failed promotion attempt, Faust had stolen his own personnel file. In that file he'd found a letter his father had written during Faust's first week of employment.

Victor Faust had been a respected man at Revenue Canada; knowing that, he'd written, "Though basically a good boy, Kelly has been emotionally troubled since his mother abandoned him when he was six years old. He's been under psychological care and is thought to be non-violent now, especially if not overwhelmed with responsibilities."

The note had enraged Faust. His mother hadn't abandoned him, she'd abandoned her husband, nor had he ever been under psychological care; but his father's statement, the implication that his son was an emotional time bomb, had effectively sabotaged any hope of a promotion to the top ranks. The report was Victor Faust's revenge on his son for deserting him as abruptly as his wife had done.

The old boys who'd worked with his father, the men who'd hung onto their clout, had neither forgotten or forgiven his insubordinate behaviour during his first years here, and his apathy later on; however, the letter in his file had motivated Faust to cultivate a better image. He joined committees, socialized with colleagues, and worked hard enough to obtain a position in Special Investigations. He'd even kept his father's picture on his desk to give the illusion of some fondness for the old man.

Once Faust realized he'd never play a vital role here, he decided to use his skills against his employers. Any promotion bid was essentially for sport now, a way of showing colleagues he still cared about this job. It was important for people to think he cared about this job.

As Faust's phone rang he stared at his father's photograph. Victor was wearing the same ugly brown suit he'd worn most of his life. The old bastard stood there: rigid, obedient, proud, and stupid.

"Hello?" He turned away from the photo and listened carefully. "Are you sure Jillian's been kidnapped?"

"Two hours have gone by and there's still no word from her," his caller replied.

"Damn it! Why didn't you get rid of her when I asked you to?"

"I've been trying to persuade her to leave, subtly."

"You're a Silby & Morrow partner. Can't you just fire her?"

"She's in a strong position here. Too many questions would be asked and I don't need more problems now. Besides," the partner hesitated, "I'm not sure it's necessary. Jillian doesn't understand what she saw, and she can't connect either of us to Ice Craft."

"She knows my name, thanks to you, and if Alex Bellamy learns about me then we've got trouble."

"Why? He can't prove anything from your end, can he?"

Faust wasn't sure. He looked at his father's face, at ferocious pig eyes dulled by years of paperwork.

"Go through her desk and see if you can find a clue to her whereabouts. Also, keep a close eye on your partners. It shouldn't be hard to learn if one of them knows more than he should about her disappearance."

"Should I watch anyone in particular?"

Faust stared at his father. "Watch them all."

"I'm worried about Tony Barker. What if he starts to resent our part in the fraud? He could call the police, hand them the Lions financial statements, and plead ignorance."

"He won't. Mr. Barker's a rich man with some rather strange income tax returns and a stranger lifestyle. In fact, I've hired Sam Roche to find out how he spends his free time."

"We can't trust Roche!"

"He's just an insurance policy. By paying him to perform a service we'll make him feel important and protected."

"Since when do his feelings count?"

"Since he became my enemy." Faust examined his manicured fingernails. "The only way to beat an enemy these days is to turn him into a weapon, then program him to self-destruct."

"Will you be programming me too?"

"Will you give me a reason to?"

The line was silent.

"Call me when you know something." Faust hung up and opened Alex Bellamy's personnel file.

Jillian was with Alex, he was sure of it. Their simultaneous disappearance was too coincidental. How had Alex learned about Jillian's connection to Ice Craft so quickly, though? Something was wrong. There was an unknown piece floating around the perimeter, a third factor working against him, and Faust knew he'd have to find the missing piece soon. If he was one of those about to lose his job, there'd be little time to complete his plan.

Faust gazed at Alex's résumé and reference letters, and at a performance report on his first six months with Revenue Canada. He picked up the chocolate éclair and began to absorb every word on young Mr. Bellamy.

SIX

Sam Roche hid at his usual spot in Alfred Lin's hedge. From this vantage point he'd taken dozens of photographs of Alfred and Marlena Margolin in bed. He'd taken photographs of them taking photographs of each other, and had thought about taking dozens more because Mrs. Margolin's talents were boundless. She could play a sleazy whore or the epitome of virtue with a skill not found in amateurs.

He remembered meeting her once at the Silby & Morrow office. She wasn't married then, but Jerry was obviously in love with her. At the time Sam had been envious; now he felt sorry for the guy.

Marlena had her back to Sam. He waited for her to turn around. She waited for Alfred.

♦ ♦ ♦

The bedroom in the mansion's west corner became humid because of the jacuzzi in the adjoining room. Added to the humidity were the aromas from Marlena's collection of lotions. She sat in the middle of the bed, massaging long tanned legs with golden ginger droplets that oozed over her knees and down the ridge of bone. Her diamond rings sparkled. Her tan grew darker and glossier under the oil. She was a perfect pearl lying on a bed of black velvet; a work of art; a portrait; the lover men wanted.

The inside of her legs tingled from spirals drawn with the tips of pink fingernails. Marlena hummed while she played. Her eyes closed as she uncapped another scent and dabbed the lime and coconut fragrance onto her shoulders. She rubbed the oil onto her breasts and was awed by the rawness of her own touch. She struggled to avoid her nipples. Temptation burned her skin. It was not yet time.

To divert herself, she opened her eyes and gazed at a bedroom swirling with glass, plants, and brass. Flowering bonsai formed a semi-circular display around a silver chess table. A game was in progress; each crystal chess piece manipulated to block its opponent. Through the window, refracted sunlight created small rainbows inside some of the pieces.

Across the room, a ten panel lacquer screen from Vietnam filled the wall. Its borders were inlaid with mother-of-pearl, gold, and ivory. Farms and airborne birds coloured buff, green and aubergine stretched across the panels where tiny weathered farmers stood beside hand-painted huts or tended miniature gardens. The village was embedded in twenty layers of a brown-black lacquer called San Canh Gian, the colour of a black beetle's wing. As a craftsperson, Marlena appreciated the intricacies necessary to create a rich, harmonious camouflage over common wood.

She shook her long dark red hair so it tickled her back and shoulders. Refilling her champagne glass, she sipped and swayed, then retrieved her kimono from the floor. Ceremoniously, she draped it over her legs and allowed herself to become spellbound by the vital dragon god embroidered on the back.

The creature's red, orange, and yellow body turned violet at the end of a long wavering tail. Taunting green and silver eyes bulged out of its satanic head and a fine silvery blue mesh glistened in the web of two small wings. A row of jade scales followed the animal's backbone as it rose from strong, tense haunches preparing to strike. Its body was stunning, its boldness immense, and it emitted a blinding spray of flame from a greedy blood red mouth whenever its deception worked, and its deception always worked here. Only after admirers had been mesmerized by the dragon's beauty and power, did they notice that it was poised to attack. In the dragon, Marlena saw her core: stark, half mad and compelling. She buried her face in the flame and didn't dare move until Alfred appeared in the room.

Water rippled down his body. Black satiny hair was swept back from his face. He walked towards her, scowling, formidable: willing her to the edge of the bed. Kneeling before Marlena, Alfred stroked unctuous demon legs. He took her kimono and tossed it on the floor.

He leaned closer to Marlena's legs until he could feel his own breath upon them. Placing his hands between her knees, he spread her thighs apart. The heat intensified with his slow climb upward. Probing fingers became wet and frantic while legs spread further and further apart.

Alfred's eyes met Marlena's half-closed eyes that reflected the understanding between them. There was no life beyond this room; just two people, a beetle-wing screen and a shared fantasy; a fantasy in which both would have to stay winners. They played the game in silence so neither could know the other too well. This was the only rule they'd set for themselves; everything else was permitted. Which was why he kissed and licked Marlena's lotions with such a desperate thirst, and why she thought she would live forever, until Alfred buried his face in the flame.

SEVEN

Alfred's chubby, middle-aged housekeeper smiled at Sam flirtatiously. "Mr. Lin'll be with you in a minute."

Sam winked at her, then strolled around the living room examining Alfred's flimsy furniture and the Chinese drawing he used to keep in his office. It was a dumb picture of purple trees. Once, Sam remarked that leaves were green and stems were brown in China same as anywhere else, but Alfred had looked at him as if he'd smeared his face with bird shit. He always looked at Sam this way.

From their first meeting Alfred made it clear that Sam had only been hired to repay a favour to a mutual friend. Alfred rarely acknowledged his presence, and spoke Cantonese to his staff and customers whenever possible. Sam ignored his rudeness because he needed the job badly. Poker, blackjack, craps, and roulette had become his favourite diversions, and as long as people lent him money, Sam played. When his debts grew larger than his salary, Sam became desperate for cash. He got it by befriending Alfred's bookkeeper.

The woman was young, inexperienced, overworked, and since Sam knew how to keep a set of books, he humbly offered his assistance. Within days, she was discussing the business with him, including the fact that Alfred's father-in-law and two uncles owned forty-nine percent of Ice Craft Jewellers. It didn't take Sam long to gain access to company records.

It took even less time to sabotage the bookkeeper's work. In three months, Sam had her job and a larger salary. He'd also hoped to have her fired, but Alfred blamed himself for overloading the woman and made her Sam's assistant instead.

Silently, methodically, the bookkeeper built a case against Sam and, over time, Alfred began to demand explanations for many transactions. Sam managed to bluff his way out of tricky situations, but impatient, self-righteous Alfred wasn't stupid and Sam knew he'd be fired soon. He had nightmares about a future with more debts and more borrowing, until he came up with a plan.

Intrigued by Tony Barker's ability to provide Ice Craft with precious stones on short notice, Sam tried to locate the source of his supply; having failed, he figured Tony was into something illegal. When Tony agreed to sell a hundred and fifty thousand dollars worth of precious stones to Ice Craft, provided Sam stopped prying into his business affairs, Sam knew he'd been right. By mutual consent, he'd planned to return most of the stones and twenty percent of the cash to Tony; however, Kelly Faust's discovery of their scheme had changed things. Faust's silence wasn't cheap. His request, though, that Sam "closely monitor" Tony's activities had already exposed valuable secrets; the kind that could secure Sam's future.

Once Sam also started spying on Alfred, for his own amusement and self-preservation, it didn't take long to realize his employer's self-righteousness was as phony as his success. Still, with the threat of jail haunting him, Sam had decided to make a deal with Alfred. Now was the perfect time to propose it, while the jerk was still sex-drenched and sleepy.

"Alfred." Sam tried to relax but Alfred's eyes were murderous. "Did I catch you at a bad time?" He knew Marlena was still here and smiled innocently. "I've found a solution to your financial problems."

"I thought I told you that you're finished at Ice Craft." Alfred's voice was hollow, his rage barely contained. "I want my office keys back. Now!"

"Alfred, listen a minute. I can help the company."

As Alfred stepped closer, Sam felt the hatred that wished him on the floor and slithering under the door.

"I know I've made mistakes, which is why I want to help you," he added hastily. "Tony fired the person who issued the phony invoices, and he wants to reimburse you by investing in Ice Craft. He's talking about a million bucks in cash, Alfred."

He wasn't sure how long it had taken Alfred to realize that the invoices weren't phony and that Sam had actually been on a buying spree, but it wasn't smart to admit the truth now.

"It's a good deal, Alfred, considering that Ice Craft only lost a hundred and fifty grand."

Alfred struck Sam across the face. He struck him repeatedly until Sam hit the floor. Alfred stepped on his abdomen. Instantly, the pressure was off and Sam was on his feet, his head yanked back by his hair, his cheeks flaring in swollen patches.

"You don't exist anymore!" Alfred yelled.

Sam broke from his grasp, scrambled over the coffee table and raced for the door. Before he could get out, Alfred had caught him, wrapped one hand around his neck, pinned him against the door with the other and raised a knee to his groin. Sweat dripped from Sam's face and trickled down the sleeve of Alfred's robe.

Alfred squeezed his neck, then released his grip.

"What if I," Sam gasped, "got the stones Ice Craft paid for?" He took a deep breath. "Tony would either have to give them to you or risk a lawsuit, right?"

Alfred glared at him.

"I found out how and where Tony has access to a hell of a lot of gems." Sam watched him carefully. "I could get them for you."

"I don't want you doing anything for me. Now get out!"

The left side of Sam's upper lip arched over his gums.

"When's your wife due back from Malaysia?"

"That has nothing to do with you."

"Yeah. I guess it only concerns you, your father-in-law and the Margolins, of course." He smirked at Alfred's blank expression. "You see, I have photographs of you and Marlena taking incredibly rude pictures of each other. So, what's it going to be? A deal with Tony for your company, or a deal with me for your marriage?"

Shadows crept over Alfred Lin's face.

"A three-way partnership with you, me and Tony would be nice. Shall we do that, Alfred, because I've got the dirtiest pictures—"

Alfred slammed his knee into Sam's groin. He yanked him away from the door, opened it, and tossed him outside. As Sam tried to stand, Alfred kicked him in the ribs and stomach. He grabbed Sam's arm and dragged him along the gravel driveway, dumping him next to his car on the street.

Sam staggered to his feet. "What's going to happen when your uncles and your father-in-law find out you squandered their money?" He took a deep breath and spit out, "because you were too busy screwing someone else's wife to pay attention to business!"

Alfred tore after Sam but he was already in the car. He waved to Alfred as he sped down the street, and wondered how to approach Tony without getting the crap beat out of him again.

EIGHT

Jillian's happiness floated through the cave, settling over passions tempered and drowsy as she reached for her lover. Nothing disturbed their peace. No music or motion, hardly an exhaled breath. Jillian waited for the sound of his breathing. The silence became unwelcome, eery. Fear pricked her senses alert. Her defenses crumpled like onion-skin paper as the hollowness crept in and bore down on her shoulders, paralyzing her torso, crushing her face.

She called to her lover for help, watched him roll slowly towards her, and when she saw his face she screamed. His cheeks were covered with raw open sores and boils oozing yellow pus. His skin had darkened into a coarse ocher stain.

Underneath, muscles convulsed grotesquely. Eyes flashed green, red, and black like frenzied strobe lights until they slowed down and stopped, and she recognized Tristan's face.

As he laughed, brown slimy particles slid over his lips. Smaller broken pieces stuck to his chin and solidified like barnacles. His eyes were sparkling black crystals penetrating her brain, vivisecting her thoughts into spineless compartments. Feelings were stripped open, beaten senseless. She couldn't stop him from touching her.

Les appeared in the cave and dictated to Jillian in low, saturnine tones. "Do this — do that — be good — be back" over and over again. He wouldn't help her, would scarcely look at her. Emptiness invaded Jillian's lungs and hampered her breathing. She heard footsteps approach — more evil was coming. There was no escape! Too many — too strong! Her rib cage seized and blew apart — seized and blew apart.

Jillian leapt out of the nightmare covered in sweat. A brilliant white ball of light swung in front of her and she covered her eyes, praying the nightmare would disappear. Her tormentor held the ball of light in his hands. She looked for solid ground but the bottom was too far away. If she leaned over much further she'd fall head first into a cracked and empty swimming pool. Jillian sat up. Her feet touched the ground. A cockroach scuttled across the floor.

"Jillian?"

The voice was familiar. She hugged herself as the light drew nearer.

"Jillian, I won't hurt you. You're safe here."

She swung her legs onto the cot and scrunched against the wall. "What happened?"

"You fainted and I brought you here." Alex put the lantern down. "You were out a long time. I was getting worried."

He held an ice bucket containing a bottle of wine. A light brown corduroy jacket partially hid his bloodstained sweat shirt. Bandages covered the cuts on his cheek.

"Where am I?" She glanced around a small, damp room swallowed by shadows. "What is this place?"

"Have some wine to relax," he replied softly.

Alex uncorked the bottle and removed two plastic cups from his pockets. He sat next to Jillian as she clasped trembling hands around the cup. The place reeked of mould and decay. In the lantern's light she saw moist and blistered walls dripping into a misshapen puddle of muck on the linoleum floor.

"Where the hell are we?"

"A tunnel under the Carnegie Centre." Seeing her confusion, he added, "It's the old Edwardian structure at the corner of Main and Hastings Street."

"We're underground?" she asked, her voice rising in pitch.

"Afraid so. The Centre was built shortly after the turn of the century, but I'm not sure if this tunnel's that old."

Her gaze darted from wall to wall. "Why build one at all?"

"Since Chinatown's a neighbour, that's a good question. People once believed the Chinese had built tunnels to hide from police raids on opium dens and gambling houses, but I don't know if the tunnels really existed. This one only goes as far as this building, and if it did connect to others it doesn't now."

Again, Jillian surveyed the room. "Oh God, I've gone to hell without dying."

"I know it seems that way, but at least no one can find us here."

Her eyes grew larger: cautious and fearful. "Why don't we want to be found?"

He hesitated. "That's not easy to answer."

Alex had found Andy's body. After he was attacked behind the apartment building, the manager had let him back inside, then into Andy's apartment when he wouldn't answer the door.

His cut cheek burned as he recalled the blood that had seeped over the quilt Ida Gowan had sewn for her son. It had swallowed the blues, greens, corals, and yellows until the fabric was a red wet sponge, and Andy's face nothing more than a waxy, bluish grey mask. The manager, pressing a handkerchief to his nose, had thought his suicide was disgusting.

"Can I get you anything?" Alex asked. "You still look a little pale."

In the lantern's light, a small gold cross flickered around his neck. She stared at him. He was too courteous to be terrifying, and stupid if he thought she'd be fooled by friendliness again.

"You can get me out of this hellhole." She scratched her arms, certain that vermin were burrowing through her dress. "Why have you been calling me?"

"Calling you?" Alex frowned. "When?"

"This morning and every night for a week." She shivered, then sipped the wine to calm herself. "Why didn't you say anything?"

"Jillian, I didn't call. I swear I don't want to hurt you."

"Fine." She sprang off the cot. "I'll go home and forget the whole thing."

"I wouldn't go out there. The tunnel's pretty rude in places, and I've had to put mouse traps in the makeshift bathroom."

Jillian gulped the wine down. "How long do you plan to keep me prisoner?"

"You're not a prisoner, you're a free person without options right now; there's a difference. Tell me about the phone calls you've been getting." Alex waited, but she didn't respond. "You panicked in the storage room because you thought I was the caller, right?"

She glared at him.

"You could have done worse," he said. "Other people have."

"What's worse than this?"

"Death."

Monty and Ida Gowan had spent three tortured days trying to find a reason for what they believed was their son's suicide. Ida asked Alex about the cuts on his face, and grew suspicious when he told her the attack happened the night Andy died. Alex wished he could tell them more, but until he could prove the Ice Craft fraud was real, no one, including the cops, would believe Andy's death was about keeping a fraud covered up.

The cops would ask a lot of questions, probably call his supervisor who'd demand that he return the files; but showing up for work was too risky if someone on the inside was involved in this.

"I'm not worth any money," Jillian said.

"I don't want money."

She kept her eyes on him. "I'm not helping you with any kinky perversion!"

"Stop yelling. You'll bring the tunnel down."

"Oh, really?" She slammed her three inch heel into his foot.

Alex moaned at the sharp pain and hobbled forward as she ran for the door. She started to open it when he yanked her back. As he spun Jillian around, she drove her fist into his stomach. Alex buckled over. Grabbing her arms, he pulled her on the floor with him. Jillian kicked, wriggled and shoved until she was exhausted and nauseated.

"Let go of me!"

"Then quit fighting!" Alex lifted her onto the cot and flopped down beside her. With one hand wrapped around her wrists, he adjusted his glasses and shifted the pager clipped to his belt.

"What a hostile woman."

"Who wouldn't be in my place?"

He stood up and, stepping away from Jillian, adjusted the pistol tucked in back of his blue jeans.

"Oh no, my dress is filthy." She stared at the black smudges and streaks.

"I'll buy you a new one."

Jillian looked at him curiously. "Are you really with Revenue Canada?"

"Yes." Dizziness blurred Alex's vision. His head began to pound. "I'm on a special investigation, sort of."

She gazed at the wall, then swiftly turned back to face him. "I only filed my tax return one day late! Or was it the hundred bucks I didn't claim for typing a friend's thesis?"

"We're not investigating you." Alex's swollen smile twisted to one side. "We're interested in a partner at your firm, but we won't know who it is until you answer a few questions."

"You've got to be joking."

"I wish I was," he said with his cheek still burning, "but the best jokes are taken and you wouldn't want to hear what's left."

"I don't know anything about the partners' tax returns."

"This isn't about tax returns. It's about a conspiracy to cover up a fraud involving Ice Craft Jewellers and Lions Imports. I'm wondering if you know something about it."

After Andy's murder, Alex had called Tristan Wells to see if he'd found any proof to substantiate a fraud conspiracy, and was told a Silby & Morrow partner might also be involved in the scheme. Tristan said that when he'd first arrived at Ice Craft, Sam Roche had told him to talk to the Silby & Morrow partners. He'd implied one of them would handle the situation but he wouldn't say which one. Tristan hadn't yet come up with evidence against any partner.

"I've heard rumours about a fraud, but I don't know anything," Jillian said. "Nothing's been proven and no one's been arrested that I know of."

"My colleague, Andy Gowan, and I were close to putting the pieces together when we were taken off the audit." After describing their abrupt removal from the case, he said, "Maybe you know more than you think you do, like who might be involved."

She shook her head.

"Then how do you explain what's been happening to you? The anonymous calls and the stuff you keep losing?"

She looked at him pensively. "Who told you I lost things?"

"A couple of people."

After talking to cooperative Silby & Morrow employees, Alex had learned a number of things about Jillian, and about some internal problems in the firm. Tristan had been especially helpful.

"You're the only employee who's been around long enough to know the partners well, and as the senior partner's secretary you have access to more information than most of the staff. I think you've been harassed because of something you saw or heard. The anonymous calls seem to support my theory."

Light green eyes widened with disbelief. Even when Jillian was terrified, angry, or skeptical, Alex thought she was beautiful. Her nose and mouth were tiny, her skin pale ivory and swirled with pink. A light spray of freckles covered her cheekbones. He watched her gaze into the distance, lost in thought.

"Hello?" Alex waved at her. "Are we open for business?"

"You're nuts."

"Not nuts, just desperate."

"Can't you talk to the partners?"

"You're the safest option I have right now."

He'd tried to contact Roche and Barker to talk about Andy's murder and the assault on himself. He'd hoped their reactions would give something away, maybe inspire dialogue intended to keep themselves from being implicated in these crimes, but neither man had returned his calls. It now seemed the only way to start solving the fraud and Andy's murder was to find out which Silby & Morrow partner had known about Roche's scam all along. Right now, he had no idea what he'd do with the information when he got it.

Alex turned to Jillian, who was leaning over the cot and tracing the neck of the wine bottle with her fingertips. Swiftly she lifted the bottle out of the bucket.

Alex grabbed it from her. "Bottles make lousy weapons," he said, "unless secretarial school taught you how to smash it over the boss's head."

"Kidnapping's against the law, and I'll press charges if I'm not out of here soon."

"The law doesn't come into it, yet. Not until I can give

them hard evidence of fraud." He put the bottle on the ground.

"I have to go home," she said urgently. "You can keep me hostage in my apartment, okay?"

"You can go when I have the information I need." He gazed at her, tempted to brush the hair from her eyes. "It's up to you."

"My mother calls nearly every day, and if I'm not there it won't be long before she calls the cops."

"I'll make sure you get in touch with her. Tell me about the phone calls you've been getting."

Jillian rolled her eyes in exasperation. "Late night calls at my place six times a night every night for the past week. No voice on the other end, sound familiar?"

Alex placed his hand on hers. "Someone's been trying to scare you."

"And here you are, what a surprise." She lifted his hand away.

"I don't think it's safe for you to go home."

"You can't force my cooperation, can you?"

Slowly Alex stood up and shuffled out of the room. He returned moments later with a shopping bag full of clothes and Jillian's purse. Jillian backed against the wall, afraid of what he'd do next.

"I stopped at your place on the way here and picked up a few things."

Her eyes narrowed. "How did you know where I lived?"

"From your driver's license. Your keys were also in your purse."

She frowned. "I didn't have my purse with me. I wanted to get it, remember?"

"I got it for you."

"How?"

"I'll tell you when you give me the information I need."

"Looks like you've planned this rather well."

He gazed at her. "I'm not even sure bringing you here

was the right thing to do, but I've been too busy to come up with a better plan."

A lime green turtle with huge black eyes peeked out of the bag. The stuffed toy had been a lucky charm for Jillian over the years. She removed the turtle and found her copy of *Pride and Prejudice*. It appeared that Alex had been in her bedroom and had gone through her things. There were socks and underwear in the bag: blue jeans, two blouses, her new white running shoes and a bulky grey cardigan. As Jillian pulled the cardigan out of the bag, two Kleenex tissues tumbled from the pockets.

"I'm not sure why I brought the turtle," Alex said, then hesitated. "I liked the puppets in your sewing basket. Is puppet-making your hobby?"

Jillian didn't answer; she was studying her watch. "It's five to twelve. You said you'd be at work this afternoon."

His smile was brief. "I lied: sorry. Would you like some lunch? There are take-out restaurants and a couple of good bakeries nearby."

She folded her arms. "April Fools' Day is supposed to end at noon. Tristan put you up to this, didn't he?"

"What?"

"This is his big joke for good old Jillian, the office dartboard. He'll come through that door yelling April Fools and then I'll gouge his eyes out!"

Alex's concerned expression irritated her. He became repulsive, his courtesy a farce. She narrowed her eyes until the green became a thin fluorescent line.

"This is real, Jillian. I'm sorry, but I can't make it go away."

"Get out!"

"I'll leave the lantern for you." He took a flashlight from his jacket pocket and opened the door. "I hate guns!" she shouted. "Don't ever point one at me again!"

Alex turned around.

"I had a bad experience once," she added.

She was eleven years old when neighbourhood punks got hold of a pellet gun and decided to have some fun. She hadn't been able to run fast enough. Jillian remembered searing pains over her back; wounds and blood on her arms; a trip to the hospital; tests and x-rays and whispered conversations; a summer ruined.

"I'm really sorry. I've never used one on a person before. Can't believe I actually did it." He watched her carefully. "If there's anything I can get you: an extra blanket, pillow, or food, just let me know."

"You can take me home, please?"

"The more I think about it, the more convinced I am that you'd be safer with me."

"One crank caller doesn't mean I'm in any danger, Alex."

"You want to stake your life on that?" When she didn't respond, he said, "Let's just do it my way, okay?"

She shut the door in his face, then folded her arms and stared at the sleeping bag on the cot. A blue pillowcase decorated with embroidered flowers offered little cheer in this dismal cage.

To keep busy, Jillian emptied the shopping bag. She put on her black blouse, blue jeans and cardigan, intending to return to work dressed this way so everyone would know what Tristan had done, the jerk.

She checked her purse to see if anything was missing, then brushed her hair and sprayed herself with cologne. She squirted the room to cover the mouldy smell. Absently, she caressed the turtle until she noticed her watch. It was twelve-twenty. Jillian tiptoed to the door and tried to open it but it was locked.

"Alex?" she called. "Alex! Oh great." She gazed around the gritty little room with its wine bucket and plastic orange cups abandoned like toys in a playpen.

Hugging her lucky turtle, she rocked back and forth on her heels, wishing Tristan would come and explain all the jokes she'd never understood; tell her it was nothing personal, that she just happened to be a better target than the broad side of a barn or a wall of balloons.

If Mom found out about the kidnapping she'd have a fit: rock back and forth, just as Jillian was rocking now. She stopped herself. Mom must never know about today: couldn't be allowed to build a case for bringing her daughter home. She had to get out of here fast: get things back to the way they were before this morning and pretend nothing had happened.

Lying down on the cot, Jillian stared at the lumpy ceiling, afraid some blob of jelly would fall on her face. If something like that had to happen to anyone it would happen to her. She was the puckered sleeve in a dress, the muddied oil portrait, the chipped piece of porcelain. She was probably done for in this smelly hellhole. Small wonder she found herself crying in the silence.

◆ ◆ ◆

The quickest route to get inside Carnegie Centre was through the tunnel, then into the back rooms and finally into the main area. During office hours, however, Alex used the alley behind the building, then walked down East Hastings Street and entered through the front doors.

Today, he strolled through the main entrance, then headed for the pay phone in an alcove on the building's north side. He dialled Silby & Morrow's number, said the call was personal and was immediately connected to Les Silby.

Alex watched people wander past the Centre's reception desk while Les reported that Martin Sloane had found blood and files on the storage room floor, and wanted to call the police about Jillian's abduction.

"You kidnapped my secretary, didn't you, Alex?"

"For a short while."

"Bring her back, *now*."

"Jillian's in trouble, Les." Alex noticed an old man with long white hair sitting nearby and watching him closely. He turned his back on the man. "Did you know she's been getting anonymous phone calls?"

Les paused. "I'm calling your superiors."

"Andy's dead. Murdered minutes before someone ambushed me. The guy wasn't after money. I think he wanted the Ice Craft files: either them or me."

Les's voice was calm. "Did you get a look at him?"

"He wore a wool face mask." Alex picked at the bandage on his face. The skin underneath was itchy. "The guy who attacked me could also be after her."

"Why?"

"Our offices are connected to the same fraud."

While Alex explained his theory about Jillian stumbling across something incriminating at the office, he gazed at three stained-glass windows. According to the labels below each window, the glass depicted portraits of Scott, Burns, and Moore. The windows shared the wall with the pay phone and were partially hidden under a spiral staircase.

"Les, I want you to play up the kidnapping angle and see what happens."

"Where are you now?"

Alex hesitated. "At a community centre."

"Which community centre?"

He glanced at the people in the reception area and listened to voices near the reception desk. "It doesn't matter. Hopefully, we won't be staying long."

"How's Jillian?"

"Furious and uncooperative, which is understandable." He propped his foot on a bench next to the phone. "Did you find the Lions Imports financial statements?"

"Jillian was looking for them when you took her," he answered icily.

"By the way, I'd still like to see your files on the company."

"I'll think about it. In the meantime, what should I tell Martin?"

Once they'd agreed on a plan, Alex hung up and wandered around the reception room, observing people and trying not to look too anxious or inept. He gazed at large stained-glass portraits of Milton, Shakespeare and Spenser overlooking the staircase between the first and second floors, and tried to guess what lay behind their serene expressions. It took a special kind of talent to determine the lies from the truth in calm faces, a talent he wished he had.

NINE

Les checked the time. It was 1:15.

He watched his partners enter the boardroom. Martin was already here, standing at attention like a soldier crammed into a sentry box.

Isobel sat apart from the others. She gave Les a brief smile and turned away.

Twenty years ago, as a young articling student, Isobel had depended on him heavily, especially during her clashes with John Morrow who did not welcome ambitious women into this office. When John died and Les made Isobel a partner, she no longer needed a mentor. She was her own answer now, cool and self-possessed, witty, charming, and after all these years, Les was still attracted to her.

He regretted that he'd allowed their friendship to dissolve into a comfortable, stale acquaintance. He didn't know how to tell her that most of the women he'd known in his life were better people than the men could hope to be.

Les didn't think she or Martin would do anything to harm the firm. Despite his argumentative nature, Martin Sloane was a loyal company man. Craig and Jerry, though, hadn't been with the firm long enough to prove a lasting commitment. Both men had acquired bad habits from previous employers and both had let their personal lives interfere with their work.

Craig gazed at the cigarette pack Isobel removed from

her purse.

"I know a stripper who smokes those. She dances with a boa constrictor that slithers over her breasts and down her belly. It's rather arousing." He smiled at her. "I keep a pet boa at home, did you know?"

"I didn't even know you danced."

"Can we get on with this?" Martin glared at Les, who rose slowly.

"I received a phone call this morning, informing me that Jillian has been . . . that someone's holding her hostage for ransom. He's calling again at 1:30. I thought you people should be present."

Expressions were momentarily suspended; the boardroom was transformed into a wax museum where blank eyes didn't move. While Martin patted his breast pocket, Jerry got up and hurried to the phone.

"What are you doing?" Les asked.

"Making sure my wife's safe." He returned Les's stare. "What if this maniac wants two victims?"

Les removed his glasses. "It's almost 1:30. I think you should wait."

Behind him, the room was silent. He watched the receiver in Jerry's hand, saw it start to rise, then waver. Gently, he put it down.

"I gather police intervention is out of the question," Isobel said.

"It's not out of the question." Martin looked at Les. "They've been notified, haven't they?"

"I was told," Les replied as he put his glasses back on, "that Jillian would be killed if the police got involved."

Craig removed his wedding ring and pressed it between his hands. "Maybe it's a hoax. She could be in on the whole thing."

Les gave him an icy look. "If you knew Jillian, you wouldn't be accusing her of this now."

"Maybe we should hire a private detective to help us,"

Isobel suggested.

"We can't afford one!" Martin's budget didn't include detectives' fees. "We have to call the police."

"It's too dangerous," Les insisted.

Jerry touched his partner's shoulder. "We'll get her back, Les."

"How? By sitting around with a finger up each other's ass?" Craig looked at Isobel.

"No wonder you get so little work done," she murmured.

"Oh, the work gets done, when it isn't being sabotaged."

"I know the feeling."

"What are you two talking about?" Martin yelled. "The issue here is kidnapping!"

"I thought it was assholes." Craig smiled at Isobel, who lifted her middle finger and twisted it back and forth.

She and Craig had adopted several similar gestures. There was a whole repertoire for young accountants who thought working for a woman was funny, or easy, or degrading. Isobel never shouted; it wasn't necessary. She used her body because men paid attention to it, although the years had taught Les to politely avert his eyes.

The telephone rang; the museum exploded with noise. Wax melted inside everyone's clothing while their expressions were again locked into place.

Les used the speaker phone. "Yes?"

"One million dollars in small bills," Alex demanded. "Put the money in a back-pack, then take it to the southwest corner of Main and Hastings. Deliver the cash alone, Silby."

"When?"

"You'll be called tonight."

The line went dead.

Martin dashed to the phone and dialled zero. "Connie! Did you get that caller's name — You idiot!"

Les yanked the phone out of his hands. "Enough! Sit down and shut up!"

The partners looked as if they'd been splashed with cold water. Les had never spoken this harshly before. In fact, he rarely raised his voice. He had another method: a blunt, derisive cynicism.

"Sorry," he mumbled.

No one spoke for several seconds. Faces were scratched, clothing adjusted, watches wound and eyeglasses cleaned. Those standing up sat down, those sitting down stood up. Les looked for one out of step with the chorus line, but everyone was upset; he had upset them.

"Was it the same voice you spoke to this morning?" Isobel asked.

"I think so."

Craig stuck his wedding ring on his thumb. Soon the band was rolling on the carpet. He crawled under the coffee table and stayed there a long time.

"Poor Jill," Jerry whispered.

"Leslie," Martin said calmly, "you must find her. The money might not make a difference."

Everyone looked at Martin. He had struck his blow. The score was even.

"If the drop-off point is Main and Hastings," Jerry stated, "then she could be in one of the nearby hotels."

Isobel turned to Craig. "Isn't that your part of town, where the boas slither?"

He gazed at her. "The local guys usually know what's going on. Somebody might have seen something."

"I'll handle the investigation," Les stated.

"Since you do it so well." Craig lit a cigarette and blew the smoke towards him. Les inhaled as subtly and deeply as he could.

"One million dollars!" Martin's face became two round crimson patches. A hundred and fifty thousand dollars was the most he'd anticipated for a secretary.

"It does seem like a lot of money for someone we're not related to." Craig saw Les's look and was satisfied with his own strike.

"Rather than bitch about it," Isobel remarked, "let's work on getting the cash."

The partners stared at Les, threw their energy towards him in an attempt to create a titan. No one wanted to take charge of this disaster. The problem was foreign and unnatural, but they forgot that responsibility was shared in a partnership. This was their profession's cardinal rule, a vital rule because everybody made mistakes in one form or another, and Les had no intention of bearing this burden alone.

"Well?" he asked. "Let's hear some ideas."

He stepped back in order to observe each partner more closely. Conversation wound around and through his ears. Les noticed Jerry's sympathy for Jillian, and Martin's concern for reputation, while Craig sought an excuse to visit the kinds of hotels where drunks urinated in stairwells and elevators.

He listened to the group work out a means of gathering the money together. When they presented a clear and concise plan, he approved of it instantly, then adjourned the meeting while his partners gazed at him with guiltless faces.

For these people, the shock was over. There'd be no more outbursts over this issue because, crisis or not, his partners were professionals when it came to financial problem solving, which was why no one wasted precious time grieving for Jillian, or even wondering if she'd been physically harmed.

Ironically, the discipline Les demanded of these people now kept him from finding the betrayer among them. With his help, a crisis had dissolved into an ordinary partners' meeting. Les sighed and shook his head in shame.

TEN

Jillian counted six small pieces of ice floating in the bucket. She put the bottle back in the water, then tiptoed to the door and listened for Alex. Several times this afternoon he'd asked questions about the partners, but Jillian hadn't told him anything. At seven o'clock, he brought in a plate of sandwiches and left. At nine, he stuck his head inside, asked if she was all right, then left her alone again.

It was almost ten p.m. now. Jillian removed the wine bottle, then placed it and the sandwich plate beside one another on the floor. Next, she spilled the bucket's contents in front of the door. She glanced at the lantern, then gripping the bucket with both hands, she screamed.

As Alex charged in, the bucket smacked his chest. He skidded on the wet linoleum and, while trying to stay upright, was struck with the sandwich plate. As he fell, Jillian picked up the wine bottle. Alex reached for her and she smashed the bottle on his shoulder. While grabbing the lantern, she started to slip. Alex was still on his knees when she regained her footing and ran.

The tunnel was black, cold, and silent. She felt dirt and pebbles under her shoes.

Alex was shouting. Jillian's legs tingled. She forced them to move faster. The path abruptly veered to the left. She prayed for a door to crawl through. Her stomach churned and bubbled. Her body felt damp from the hours spent in this vile place. As she ran, the passage curved and swarmed over Jillian. She felt as if she'd stepped into a fairground ride where a circle of landscapes spun into a blurry paste.

She spotted a crack of grey light in the darkness ahead. As she bent before it, her lantern exposed a small wooden knob. She pulled, but the stiff warped door only widened by inches. Frantically she pulled harder, and again, until she was able to crawl through a three-foot-high opening.

In the dusty, yellow-grey light, boxes were stacked everywhere. More light shone through a high, narrow window pane on the other side of the room. While Jillian ploughed through the boxes, Alex arrived. She opened the door under the window, then charged up a long set of stairs and into an office. From there she entered a larger room filled with books, tables, and chairs.

Jillian hid at the end of a row of shelves, then spotted a reception area through a glass panel in the nearest door. She could see the main doors and, beyond, the busy intersection of Main and Hastings. She was almost free, except Alex was here.

Jillian tiptoed to a row of books closer to the exit. She bolted for the nearest door, opened it, and raced into the reception area as Alex leapt, nailing her to the floor. He clamped a hand over her mouth while Milton, Spenser, and Shakespeare watched impassively. Alex lay on top of her, his chest heaving, out of breath. He looked at the main doors to see if they'd been spotted, but the reception desk hid them from view.

Jillian tried to twist away from him. "Get off me!"

"No." He pinned her arms behind her. The perfume she wore was nice; she felt nice underneath him. "I like it here. You remind me of a girl I met on a camping trip in Luxembourg. Her hair was the same beautiful dark colour as yours, only longer."

"Alex, this floor is cold!"

He hauled Jillian to her feet, then adjusted the pistol in

his waistband while Jillian dusted off her clothes. When he tried to take her hand she pushed him away. Grasping her arm, he pulled her back through the library, then the office, and into the basement.

"You picked the wrong night to escape," he remarked. "The Centre often holds evening events."

The tunnel seemed colder, damper; the lantern was dented. Every few feet she stumbled into Alex, then shoved him away again. As they approached Jillian's room, she stumbled once more. This time, he stepped to one side and watched her hit the ground. When they entered the room, Jillian lay down on the cot and turned her back on him.

Alex sat beside her. Beads of sweat glistened under his bangs. "That was a stupid thing to do."

"I almost made it."

"Would you rather go back to anonymous phone calls?"

She turned to him. The bandages on his cheek were gone and he'd exchanged the sweat shirt for a red pull-over.

"Go to hell." She flung her lucky turtle at him.

She had spent twelve hours in this cold, stale dump. With each hour she'd grown more despondent, her ideas about his intentions more sinister. She sneezed and removed a tissue from her pocket.

"I'll bring you more sandwiches," he said.

"You can drop the nice guy act."

Slowly, Alex stood up. "And you'll eat them if I have to shove every slice of bread down your throat." He tried to scowl, but his mouth merely stretched into a long disjointed smile.

"You're not funny." Jillian rubbed her shoulder.

"Did I hurt you?"

"Yes."

"Sorry. Can I get you an aspirin or something?"

"You know what I want," she said quietly.

"And you know I can't."

"What is so difficult about opening the damn door?"

Alex hugged the turtle as he scratched the back of his hand. "There's a murderer on the other side."

The room was silent for several seconds. "Bull."

Lowering his arms, Alex held the turtle by its foot. "It's true, kind of."

"Why should I believe you? You haven't been completely straight with me so far."

Alex removed his glasses. She sounded like Andy: conservative, reticent.

"I've been honest, for the most part. Trouble is, you don't like what you've heard."

"What I haven't heard are names. Who do you suspect in the fraud, besides a Silby & Morrow partner?"

He put his glasses back on. "Sam Roche, Tony Barker, and someone in our Special Investigations Division."

Jillian grabbed the turtle from him. "You really are nuts! Revenue Canada probably fired you and this is your revenge, right? Pull a little kidnapping stunt and blame it on others. There's no way you'd be authorized to investigate like this."

"When we showed up to do the audit, Roche clearly thought there'd already been some sort of arrangement with us," Alex explained. "He also said something about a Silby & Morrow partner handling things for him." He didn't add that Roche had mentioned this to Tristan Wells. "Then there was the way we were suddenly pulled from the audit by S.I."

She stared at him. "It doesn't feel good when someone abruptly takes you off the job and shoves you aside, does it?"

Alex scratched the skin around his cuts. "I didn't realize yours meant that much to you."

"That's not it."

"What then?"

Jillian didn't want to explain her fear about inheriting her mother's agoraphobia. If she could just go outside and walk around a bit, she wouldn't feel so afraid.

"Alex, who told you to look for me in the storage room?"

"Les Silby."

"That's a lie. Les may not like government auditors, but he'd never ask one of them to meet his staff in the dungeon."

He glanced around the room, unable to think of a quick reply.

"By the way," she said, as she tossed the turtle on the cot, "where's your accomplice?"

He picked an orange cup off the floor. "Accomplice?"

"The other guy on the audit; you said his name was Andy. Does he think you're nuts too?"

"He used to." Alex gazed at the sandwiches soaking in a puddle of water. "He was murdered." He began pacing the room and said, "and I figure the people behind the fraud are responsible for his death and the assault on me."

He rubbed his left shoulder, recalling how Andy's shoulder had been stiff and sore as a result of helping him move the bookcase last weekend. The stiffness had probably hindered his ability to fight back. Guilt pushed down on Alex's shoulders. If he hadn't dropped his end of the bookcase. . . . He swung his arms in large, exaggerated circles and again pictured determined blue-grey eyes blinking at him through a face mask.

"If you don't believe me, the funeral's in two days." He looked at her. "Maybe the coffin'll be open so you can have clearer proof, not that you know what Andy looked like, but ask around. I could be lying, right?"

She picked up the turtle. "I'm sorry."

Alex watched Jillian intently, pleased to have appealed to her sympathy and mystified by Andy's power to help. "Have any partners had dealings with someone from Revenue Canada in recent weeks? I hear you have a memory for names."

"The partners don't tell me anything."

"Except for Les," he said. "I understand he was the partner in charge of Ice Craft, and that Craig McBride handled Lions Imports. I hear you do some typing for Craig, too."

She studied him. "Who's been telling you this?"

Alex's pager started beeping. "I've got to go. Should I lock you in, or will you promise to stay here?"

"I'll stay put."

"You sure?"

"I'm not a liar, Alex. Anyway, I had no plans tonight."

Her smile was hesitant and kind of snarly, but Alex was encouraged. "Aside from Les and your mom, will anyone be wondering where you are?"

She shook her head. "My friends know I'm busy these days."

"There's no special someone you've made plans with for the weekend?"

Jillian shoved her hands in the pockets of her cardigan. "I'm not seeing anyone right now, if that's what you're asking." She noticed his smile, then nodded towards the door. "How did you know about this place?"

"I worked upstairs a few years ago. The old man I replaced showed it to me."

"And the lock on my door?"

"Just a padlock bought at the store."

"So, this was all planned." She looked at the cot. "Right down to the sleeping bag and fancy pillowcase."

"Not really. I've been living down here for the last two days and didn't want someone else stealing my stuff."

"Is this tunnel that busy?"

"I guess we'll find out."

She saw his worried expression. "I don't understand why you felt you had to literally go underground."

"I don't understand why you're writing a book review on *Pride and Prejudice*." He nodded towards the novel lying on top of her dress. "I think it's already been done."

She picked at the tissues in her pocket. "Writing about books was the only thing I did well at school. I still enjoy it."

Alex walked to the door. "See you soon."

"So, what are you sleeping on?"

"A friend dropped off another sleeping bag. As for the pillow, well, I normally sleep with two."

"I hope my arrival won't cause you a pain in the neck."

Again, he smiled. "I'll manage."

As he retraced his route back to the reception-room, Alex began to feel that, just maybe, he'd come out of this okay. Once he moved Jillian above ground she might be a little more cooperative and not so desperate to go home.

After calling his answering service, Alex phoned Silby & Morrow. "Hi, what's up?"

"I found the Lions Imports audit file." Tristan's voice was hushed and excited.

"Where?"

"In the file room, exactly where it wasn't at five this afternoon. The tax returns and financial statements are missing, though."

"Does Les know?"

"Should I ask him? He's still here."

"Is anyone else?"

"Probably. People have been coming and going all night; one of the symptoms of an approaching tax season."

"Nobody's seen you with the file, I hope."

"I've been careful. Do you want the file?"

"Absolutely."

"I'll take it home. Is Jillian okay?"

"Yeah, thanks for your help."

"My pleasure. Anything else I can do?"

"Watch things, and be careful."

"I always am."

Alex listened to the line click, then heard a second click follow it. He stared at the receiver, tempted to call Tristan again, but warning him could make things more dangerous.

He looked at the marble staircase winding up and beyond

the stained-glass trio. This place had always been spooky after midnight. To relax, he'd play a radio while washing floors and emptying garbage cans. His parents never knew about his janitorial job the summer after high school graduation, or that he'd seriously considered keeping the job during a period of rebellion against the family's ambition.

Alex thought he heard something behind him. Reaching for his gun, he peered at every shadow and darkened corner. Sweat trickled down his forehead. He tiptoed out of the alcove and ran back to Jillian.

ELEVEN

Les Silby believed that people who'd never run a business didn't know a damn about anything. Les had run a prosperous practice for twenty years, and in spite of recent agitations, he thought the future looked good. In the morning, he'd tell his partners the police had found Jillian and that he'd sent her on a short recuperative vacation. He'd then order Alex to bring her back. If Alex said no, then he'd threaten to call the police. If he still said no, then he'd consider actually making the call.

Martin Sloane had barricaded himself in Les's office at five o'clock this evening to wait for the "kidnapper's" call. By the time Tristan Wells poked his head in at eight, Les had had enough company. He walked both men to the elevator, locked off access to the twentieth floor, and only then felt protected inside the "west end refuge," as his ex-wife, Anna, used to call it.

Les stared at the lights of downtown. It was late, yet other offices were lit, other people were working hard to build careers. In her good moods, Anna had called him a workaholic. In her bad moods, he was a power tripping fraud more devoted to his ego than his family. Once, in a fit of anger, Les told Anna that clients found his workaholism endearing. He said hard work and honesty were essential to improve the profession's stodgy image since a low profile didn't guarantee respectability anymore. Anna thought his ideas and ethics were a sham, and over the years her sense of humour grew more caustic while Les clung to his principles like a child to a soggy cookie. Gradually, public C.A. firms underwent the changes he wanted. An increased versatility in services boosted their fees, and the profession gained a high profile image. "Accountants," the critics wrote, "controlled the country's economy by playing billion dollar corporations against one another and collecting fees from all sides."

Small businessmen, feeling victimized by free trade, the Goods and Services Tax, and a weak economy during the last recession, began to lose confidence in their high-priced accounting experts. Consequently, Les lost a few clients about the same time Anna left the marriage. Lately, he'd begun to wonder if his principles were the sham his ex-wife had resented so much. Why else was he breaking them to save the business he told her principle had built?

Les walked away from the window, his stomach hollow, his chest thumping. Papers were heaped over his furniture, books missing from his shelves. If all went well, Jillian would be here tomorrow to restore order. Stepping across the hall, Les frowned at her desk where someone had scattered the contents of files.

He toured the floor to see if anyone was still here when a noise from the lobby smashed through the silence. Les stopped. He thought he'd heard someone cry out. Quickly, he hurried toward the lobby. When he arrived, no one was there. Someone could have tripped and fallen while stepping into the elevator. Locked access to this floor only kept people from coming up; the staff could still ride down.

On his way to the coffee room, Les noticed that the stairwell door was ajar. It was supposed to be permanently locked from the outside. Partners and senior staff had a key, though, and keys could be lent to anyone. Cautiously, Les walked up to the door and slowly pushed it open.

Martin Sloane was kneeling on the landing. He had a

file in his hands and was peering at several drops of blood surrounding a pair of black framed glasses. The glasses were missing an arm and the right lens was broken. More blood spotted the steps.

Martin looked at him. "First, I find blood and files on the storage room floor, and now this!"

Les helped him up. "What are you doing here?"

"Trying to work. I turned the elevator back on from the lobby, then came up and locked it off again. A few minutes ago, I heard a commotion and found this," he handed the file to Les, "on the floor."

It was the missing Lions Imports file. Les glanced inside the folder, then studied the broken glasses. "Who belongs to those?"

"I don't know, I didn't see anyone. We'd better call the police."

"Not yet."

"Leslie, somebody tried to steal this file and may try again! This building isn't safe."

"It might have been one of our own staff."

"Why would one of ours sneak out like this, and where is he or she now?"

"I'll look around. In the meantime, you go home and get some sleep."

Martin stared at him. "You were reluctant to call the police when I told you about Jillian's kidnapping. You were still reluctant after the ransom demand. I know you were worried about her safety, but why are you stalling now, Leslie?"

"They could ask about the significance of Lions Imports, which could lead to awkward questions about Ice Craft. Do you want that to happen?"

Martin hesitated.

"Go home, Martin."

Les wondered if his partner had another reason for staying at the office tonight, if he'd intended on taking the file himself; but why the disturbance in the stairwell? Martin wasn't hurt and didn't seem capable of physical harm. He watched him start towards the elevator, then stop and turn around.

"Has the kidnapper called?"

"No."

When he'd gone, Les telephoned Alex's answering service, then sat down and looked nervously around the reception area. The lobby was gloomy in the semi-darkness. Who wanted the Lions Imports file badly enough to risk stealing it? He tried to remember if any of his staff wore black framed glasses, and nearly jumped out of his chair when the night line rang.

"Alex!"

"Les? What's wrong?"

"I found the Lions Imports file." Les waited for his reply. "Are you there?"

"Yes."

"Martin found the file in the stairwell next to several drops of blood. I'm assuming the blood isn't yours?"

Alex paused. "It isn't."

"Ah, then it seems we have an epidemic."

"Any idea what happened?"

"None; however, he also found a broken pair of glasses on the floor and, before you ask, I don't know whose they are. Both Martin and I heard a noise, but we didn't see anyone."

"Are you sure Martin saw no one?"

Les gazed at the elevators. "You're very shrewd, Mr. Bellamy."

"What's in the file?"

"Not the financial statements and tax returns." Les rubbed his forehead. "They're probably in the hands of the damn thief."

Alex knew better than to tell him the statements hadn't been in the file. "Do you know where to get another set of statements?"

"Well, if you return Jillian, I'll have her print out another set."

"Any secretary can do that, Les. I'm surprised you didn't think of it earlier."

Les paused. "Assuming the thief isn't a staff member, the culprit must have known the floor's layout fairly well."

He suddenly thought of Tony Barker, but the man didn't wear glasses, unless he'd paid someone else to do his dirty work. Perhaps he wanted a peek at the working papers to see if disparaging remarks had been written about his company, especially where the numbers of his audited statements were concerned.

"Maybe you should clean up the blood, and save the glasses for me," Alex said. "Don't get any fingerprints on them, okay?"

"I'll think about it." Les hung up.

How he regretted Alex's involvement in the Ice Craft matter. After years of careful protection, his west end refuge was disintegrating like rice paper in a hurricane. His ex-wife would laugh and say he had it coming. His failures had been her only source of amusement during their last months together. He'd let her use them, every one of his shortcomings from eating habits to child-rearing because, all things considered, he'd probably deserved the abuse.

TWELVE

Kelly Faust walked down the street and dabbed blood from his eye with a handkerchief. The pain pierced his skull and exploded in a sunburst that only intensified his anger at failing to locate Alex Bellamy.

The door had hit him with a brutal force, injuring his cheek and brow. Blood still trickled down his face. He wasn't sure about the damage to his eye. He could see a little, but it was sore as hell.

While climbing the steps to Silby & Morrow's floor, he'd heard someone approach the exit but hadn't expected such a hostile attack. The incident, however, proved what his Silby & Morrow contact had claimed after eavesdropping on a phone conversation with Alex earlier tonight: young Mr. Bellamy had an accomplice inside the firm, someone keeping an eye on the Lions Imports/Ice Craft situation, which explained how he'd learned about Jillian's problems so quickly. She must have told someone at the office about her anonymous caller. But who would she have confided in? Tonight's setback was only temporary, though. Faust had survived worse pain than this.

The threats, humiliation, and beatings by his father had increased after his mother ran off. As a man, he could withstand any form of pain now, overcome any obstacle; certainly a bash in the eye, or unemployment. At five o'clock this afternoon, he'd learned of his own pending lay-off.

Four blocks away, Faust located a phone booth and dialled his Silby & Morrow contact's number. "I've had a slight accident and can't drive. Can you pick me up?"

"What happened?"

He mentioned the incident in the stairwell, but otherwise explained little.

"Kelly, what in hell were you doing at my office?"

"Coming to see you."

"By way of the stairwell?"

"Remember the night you first took me to your office? We used the stairs because you were afraid to be seen with me in the elevator."

"So?"

"You left your key ring on the desk while you checked to make sure we were alone. I took the key off the ring. Don't tell me you've never noticed it missing."

His contact paused for a few moments. "What did you want to see me about?"

"Two things." He dabbed at the blood still trickling into his eye. "First, did you find out who Alex Bellamy was talking to on the phone?"

"No."

"How hard did you try?"

His contact didn't answer.

"The man on the other side of the door was fairly tall, I think, with brown hair. Did you see anyone like that tonight?"

"How could I? I was in my office trying to get some work done. Were you seen in the stairwell?"

"Neither of us saw the other clearly." Faust put more pressure on his eye to stem the flow of blood. "I wish you'd recognized the voice on the phone. The man could have led us to Alex and Jillian."

"Look, it was bad enough just hiding the damn Lions file all these months, never mind putting it back, and I couldn't have spied on my staff without being recognized sooner or later!"

"Where did you put the Lions financial statements and tax returns?"

"They're with me. I'm going to create a legitimate set, then destroy the falsified documents."

"How? The originals, with your signature on them, are locked in my office."

"It's not my signature. You damn well know the firm's name goes onto audit reports," his contact answered defensively. "To protect myself, though, I forged Silby & Morrow's name in another partner's handwriting. Anyway, switching statements wouldn't be hard for you to do."

Blood oozed down Faust's hand. His handkerchief was soaked. "For now, I'd like you to keep the statements intact."

"I thought the idea was to remove ourselves from Lions Imports and Ice Craft as much as possible."

While searching for tissues, Faust pulled a blue and red ski mask out of his pocket, and placed it on the ledge under the phone. "If you keep the Lions statements in your office, it might draw the young man out again."

"I can't do that! How will it look if he finds them there?"

"Make something up. You're good at lying, my friend; very good. Now please come and get me." Faust pressed his last tissue against his eye. "I'm in a phone booth on Georgia Street, a block east of your office."

"Kelly, I can't take much more of this."

"You'll have to. As it is, certain partners suspect your integrity."

"Everyone's integrity is suspect."

"Perhaps, but yours is documented."

Again his contact hesitated. "What does that mean?"

"Just get down here. We have more business to tend to, which was my second reason for seeing you tonight."

"What business?"

"A close look at the southwest corner of Main and Hastings Streets. It's our only lead on Alex Bellamy's whereabouts." The blood-soaked tissue began to disintegrate in Faust's hand. "You said that's where the kidnapper wanted the money taken, right?"

"I can't risk being seen down there."

"I need you to identify Jillian for me."

"What for? You said you know what Alex looks like, and since you're convinced they're together. . . ." The partner's voice faded.

"Just get over here." Faust grabbed the mask and held it against his eye. "By the way, my glasses fell off in the stairwell and I'd like them back. Think you can manage it?"

The partner's moody, uncooperative silence irritated him.

"Have you heard from Sam Roche?" he added. "He's not answering my messages."

"Damn! Now what?"

"He'll have to be contacted. We can't expect all of our potential threats to commit suicide, can we?"

THIRTEEN

Asking for a receipt, Sam Roche paid the Sapphire Club's admittance fee, then sauntered into the lifestyle of his dreams. His confidence was sharp, his appetite for coy, luxurious women enhanced by Marlena's performance this afternoon. He stared at the ladies' enamelled faces, their jewellery, their short, shimmery dresses moving with the music. He ogled their bare flesh. He swooned over women with lips parted and whispering into the rims of wine glasses. Sam penetrated the room, nudging, sniffing, and brushing against scented backs and arms. He gaped at long hair and soft shoulders, and dreamed about orgies with tight silk dresses pulled high over naked hips.

The Sapphire Club exuded success as all of Tony's spots did; he had a talent for transforming other peoples' failures into profit. Four previously bankrupt restaurants were now the most popular spots in town. His restaurants weren't richly decorated, but in Tony's places old wallpaper became classic, ordinary food exotic.

While spying on Tony's house, at Kelly Faust's request, Sam saw his own fantasies focus into tangible goals, and as he learned more of Tony's secrets, Sam found himself involved in a thrilling all or nothing situation. He hadn't told Faust about his latest discovery. Sam wanted leverage against him to ensure his own success.

"Give me a bourbon."

When the bartender returned, Sam said, "I'm looking for Tony Barker; he's a friend of mine."

The drink was shoved in front of him. "That'll be fifty bucks."

"I want a receipt."

"Drop dead."

Sam pulled the money from his wallet.

"Over there." The bartender nodded to a door as Sam fastened the bills to a coaster with his chewing gum.

Behind the door, three men in ruffled blue shirts stood around a woman wearing a plunging, blue sequinned evening dress. Her feet were propped on a table, the dress split open to mid-thigh to expose a long, slinky pair of legs. One man massaged her foot. She wore a diamond and pearl choker around her neck, more jewels on her wrists. She wore her thick red hair up off her shoulders, and Sam's eyes glistened as he recognized Marlena Margolin. The men stared at Sam while Marlena gazed at the five long hairs drooping over his lip.

"Looks like Billy just made himself another forty bucks," one of the men said, then smirked.

"Fifty." Sam returned the smirk. "Is Tony around?"

"Do you have an appointment?" Marlena asked.

Sam's eyes darted over her body like a ferret on the scent of hidden prey. "We've met before, haven't we?"

"I don't think so." Her gaze tore at his eyes.

"Tell your boss, Sam Roche is here. I work for Alfred Lin."

"I'm Mr. Barker's assistant," she responded coolly. "You can leave a message with me."

Sam grinned. "I thought all assistants were dumb, ugly, and neurotic."

"I thought all men could grow moustaches." She rang Tony's office. "A Mr. Roach is here to see you. Yes, Roach, as in creepy little bug. Says he works for Alfred Lin. . . . I'll send him up."

She pointed to a staircase.

"That's Roche," Sam said, "with a soft 'o' and a nice 'shhh' sound, like you're whispering something dirty in my ear."

"Up there, Roach, and if you need help getting those spiders' legs off your lip, we've got a pair of pliers nearby."

Sam placed his glass next to Marlena's toes. Silently, he started to climb the stairs, then turned back to her.

"Tell me, Mrs. Margolin, how's Jerry? I haven't seen him in a while but I'll be talking to him soon. Count on it." His smile was rude enough to provoke a wall of ruffled shirts into charging after him.

Marlena watched Sam pound on the door. When he stumbled inside, she stood up and marched out of the room.

Tony was at his desk, writing in a ledger. The curly grey and white fringe of hair around his head had grown slightly longer since their last meeting. The tweed jacket made Tony look too large for both his chair and his desk. Sam had never seen Marlena in Tony's bedroom, but he was sure they were lovers. An accountant couldn't afford the jewellery Marlena wore, and no sane employer would give rich presents without sex in return.

"Hello, Sammy," he said cheerfully. "Help yourself to a drink. Liquor and glasses are on the bookshelf."

The room reminded Sam of a cluttered rabbit hutch full of exotic little turds. A mahogany bookcase held a collection of driftwood and splintered artifacts. A clock shaped like a dogwood blossom hung on a pine wall. Red cedar shutters covered the windows, and a pair of lamps made from fossils sat on varnished cedar tables.

Tony shut the ledger and looked at Sam. "Amazing room, isn't it? My wife wouldn't let me keep this stuff in the house, so I brought it here. Did you get a drink?"

"No." A wife? Sam hadn't spotted any wife since he began spying on Barker. He leaned towards the bookcase and searched for the liquor as he pondered this news.

"Wrong shelves." Tony walked to a second bookcase wedged between the sofa and the cedar shutters. "What would you like?"

"Bourbon." Sam started to light a cigarette.

"I'd rather you didn't smoke in here."

Sam smiled and put the cigarette away. "I have a business proposition that involves Alfred Lin."

"Really?" Tony studied him. "There isn't much left to make a proposition with, I should think."

Sam laughed. His body still ached from Alfred's attack this afternoon, but the bruises had been worth the trip.

"Alfred could use an investor in Ice Craft. For the right amount of cash, he'd probably make you a partner." Sam swallowed a third of the drink. "He needs money so badly he might offer me a similar deal, with your influence, of course."

"How much do you think he needs?"

"About a million, and seeing as how his financial problems are our fault. . . ." Sam shrugged.

"You're feeling remorseful," Tony remarked. "Since when do you have a million dollars to invest?"

"I don't, but I do have some cash, and your friendship, of course."

"What if I'm not prepared to invest a million dollars in Ice Craft?"

"Come on, Tony, I know you're a gambling man at heart," Sam replied, and smiled. "At least meet with Alfred to see if the idea's profitable. I'm sure Jerry can work out some sort of tax advantage for us, and since we're all taxed to death anyway, wouldn't that be nice?"

Tony tucked the glass under his chin as he continued to study Sam. "What makes you think I'm a gambling man?"

Sam again smiled as he recalled the first time he followed Tony out of the city, and the jackpot he'd discovered on subsequent trips.

"I'll teil you sometime, but right now I've got to go."

He opened the door, wary about meeting the ruffled shirts. "When you see Jerry, ask him for copies of Ice Craft's financial statements so you can see what a good investment it is, not that you don't already know."

Sam was well aware that Tony couldn't resist a chance to have easy access to even more precious stones, since it suited his lifestyle, not to mention his needs, so perfectly.

Tony tapped the rim of his glass as Sam opened the door and peeked outside. To his relief, the ruffled shirts were gone. Unfortunately, Marlena had gone with them. He wanted to tell her he built dreams around harlots and invite her to spend the night with him. It was almost time for a celebration, and he contemplated jubilant rites with her in a raw, hot, sweaty rhapsody.

◆ ◆ ◆

"What's Alfred doing for money these days?" Tony asked Marlena.

"We never discuss business," she replied.

Although Marlena's affair with Alfred was her own concern, Tony condoned the relationship because there were still profitable reasons for keeping Alfred within reach. Sam Roche wasn't the first person to contemplate an Ice Craft take-over. Tony knew Marlena was aware of this. He also knew she didn't particularly care.

"Does Sam know about your relationship with Alfred?"

"Possibly." She recalled the way Roche looked at her tonight, and the rage in Alfred after he had booted him off the property earlier today. "Alfred wouldn't tell me what they talked about, but I heard him yelling. If Roche knows about us then he'll have to be kept from telling Jerry. Killing the little bug would solve the problem."

Tony laughed. "I'd like to know why he thinks he's so dangerous first." He took Marlena's hand. "Listen, I have to ask a special favour of you, and I apologize for doing so."

She looked at him. "You want me to give up Alfred."

"For a while. I'm sorry."

"He won't like it."

"I know, but it wouldn't hurt you to pay more attention to Jerry. You're the only one who can convince him to join us."

"Asking him to give up a partnership to become your employee won't be easy."

"He'll be making more money and working less hours. Hell, he spends most of his time fixing my tax problems anyway. I trust the man, Marlena. I want him in charge of all of my financial affairs, including the more obscure ones."

Marlena had never asked who'd taken part in the Ice Craft fraud, but Tony assumed she knew him well enough not only to guess the truth, but also to accept it without question.

"I want Roche kept away from Jerry," she stated. "He's not to find out about Alfred, ever."

Tony smiled. Before Jerry, she'd never jumped to anyone's defense, except perhaps his own. "I'll see what I can do."

He knew Jerry Margolin had done a great deal for Marlena. He'd abolished the worst of her self-destructive tendencies; brought stability and self-esteem back to her without knowing she'd needed his help. Silly men like Sam had never been a match for Marlena, not that Sam was any match for Tony either. Tony had spent most of his life living in clouds he maneuvered. He'd never begrudged Sam's attempt to do the same, but where Tony had always known the distance between his feet and the ground below, Sam had never bothered to look. His failure, therefore, was inevitable.

Tony pressed Marlena's hands in his and gazed at her with the devotion of an old friend. "Tell me, if you were to kill Sam, how would you like to do it?"

"Slowly," she answered, "and with my eyes wide open."

FOURTEEN

Les knelt in the stairwell landing looking for signs of blood. He didn't want any stains left, any reminder that would renew Martin's panic.

"Did you lose something?" Tristan poked his head through the doorway and grinned.

"You're here early, Mr. Wells. I'm honoured."

"Yeah well, the Ice Craft files need more work."

Les stared at him. The files were complete, though. He'd glanced at them last night. Perhaps Tristan was unprepared. Perhaps he planned on photocopying the work to protect himself should numbers change mysteriously and his competency wind up challenged in court: a scapegoat for the firm.

"Les?" Jerry Margolin appeared behind Tristan. "What are you doing on the floor?"

"Looking for peace and quiet," he answered facetiously.

"I got a call from Tony last ni—"

"There you are!" Martin Sloane's crumpled brown suit squeezed between the others. He frowned at the scoured stairwell, as if irritated by the absence of blood. "Leslie, we have to talk."

"If it's about Jillian you can relax. The police found her early this morning and she's fine." He didn't like lying to his partner, but the last thing he needed was more fear and anxiety.

"Is she here?" Jerry asked.

"Not yet." Les hurried to his office, opened the door and found Craig McBride rummaging through his papers.

"I thought you should know I'll be working at home today." Craig strolled towards him. "Any news on Jillian?"

"The police found her and she's fine." Les sat in his chair. "Please don't touch anything on my desk."

Craig stared at him. "You've always said personal secrets should stay at home and professional ones should be shared, or is our senior partner the first to break his own rule again?"

Les called the receptionist. "Connie, has Isobel Cameron arrived yet?"

"She's in her office. Do you know if Jillian will be in today?"

"She's got the flu, so please take messages for me." He hung up quickly.

"Have a nice day, Les." Craig slammed the door behind him as Les's phone rang.

"Yes?"

"Les, I'd like to talk to you about Tony," Jerry said.

"Can I call you back in a minute? I have something to do first."

"Sure." Jerry hung up as his wife walked in. Without a word, Marlena chucked a file on his desk and opened her coat.

"Where's your blouse?" he asked in astonishment.

"I'm wearing one. It's just a little sheer, that's all."

He hurried to her, as a wide grin spread across his face. "There's no bra!"

Jerry wrapped his arms around his wife. He'd never understood why a woman as vital as Marlena had married someone preoccupied with the Income Tax Act; yet she'd accepted his proposal without hesitation and sometimes he felt indebted to her.

"Any word on Jillian?" Marlena asked.

"Apparently the police found her and she's okay."

"That's nice. You forgot Tony's personal tax file this morning." She nodded towards the desk. "Did you tell Les about Tony's chat with Sam Roche last night?"

"I've been trying to."

Marlena put her arms around her husband's neck. "You know, I'd love to see Roche in jail and fat ugly guys torturing his balls."

"Don't worry about it." He stroked her back. "He's no threat to us."

"He wouldn't be if you worked for Tony."

Jerry was silent.

"A two-hundred-thousand dollar a year starting salary is worth mentioning at least that many times." Marlena watched him closely. "What's holding you back?"

The thought of ending his partnership with Les bothered Jerry, but if relations between partners continued to deteriorate, the firm didn't have much of a future.

"Tony won't tell me enough about the job."

"I'll invite him to dinner and you can talk then. Tony wants to talk to you about his island."

"He already did, remember?"

"He didn't tell you he started a business there, and that it's growing fast."

"What kind of business?"

"Something big," Marlena murmured as she kissed his neck, "and terribly exciting."

◆ ◆ ◆

Les strode towards Craig's office until laughter from the students' room altered his route. A sign over the door said, "Welcome to Scuttlebutt Lodge. Visitors, please wipe your feet."

The students' room was a large windowless area built in the middle of the floor. Desks, filing cabinets, and tables filled most of the space; blackboards, bulletin boards, and cubbyholes covered the walls. Students were gathered around Tristan Wells' desk as Les stood in the doorway waiting to be noticed.

"I thought they were lying when they said they'd misplaced the cemetery's ledgers," Tristan said. "I told them it was illegal to bury records, get it?"

As the room groaned, two students spotted Les and quickly returned to their desks.

"Anyhow, plots were filling up and they wanted to know when to buy more land. So I had to count graves and see what was left. The thing is, what if a couple of bodies had been snatched to gain space so they could put off buying more land? Wooh-ooh-ooh!"

Those who hadn't seen Les started to laugh.

"Mr. Wells," Les stepped inside, "bring the Ice Craft files to my office *now*."

He wanted to leave the room but found Martin blocking the exit. Les resented his presence. It was as if the man knew when he wasn't wanted and felt compelled to appear out of defiance. As Martin marched into the room, calculators leapt into action under amused expressions. His neck stretched to a freakish length. His eyes darted over the students.

"This place is a pig sty!" Martin usually inspected the area once a day, but Jillian's abduction had ruined his schedule. "There'll be a seminar on cost benefit analysis at five o'clock Monday. I'll expect everyone there."

As Les slipped away, Martin hurried after him. "I know who had the Lions Imports financial statements last," he called out. "I know exactly where she hid them in her office."

Isobel Cameron suddenly joined them and linked her arm with Les's. "There's a client I need to discuss with you."

Ignoring Martin's contemptuous scowl, she walked Les to his office and, after closing the door, sat next to him on the sofa.

"Thanks for bailing me out." He rubbed his forehead. "Jillian's been found. I sent her away for a rest."

Isobel leaned against the sofa. "I phoned your house

until twelve last night. I was afraid something awful had happened."

"I was here."

She clasped her hands together. "Before subjecting myself to a round of Isobel-bashing, I'd better tell you that Martin did see the Lions Imports file on my desk last Thursday night."

Les watched her carefully. "Go on."

"I left my office about ten-thirty and was heading down the elevator when I remembered that I'd intended to leave an important note in a file. When I returned, I noticed that the lamp in my office had been switched on, so I tiptoed to the door to see if anyone was there."

She kept her gaze on Les. "I saw Craig slip a file under my papers. After he left, I discovered he'd given me the missing Lions file, complete with financial statements and corporate tax returns. I didn't return it to the file room until the next morning. Martin must have succumbed to one of his snooping moods some time after I went home."

"Had the statements been signed?"

"I didn't look," Isobel replied, then paused. "Les, what does the Ice Craft situation have to do with Jillian?"

She saw the alarm surface in Les's narrowing eyes. "Her disappearance is just a little too coincidental, isn't it? By the way, did you know that Craig and Sam Roche are drinking buddies?"

"I did not."

Something bumped against Les's door. The handle turned and Tristan stumbled in with a stack of files which he dumped on the coffee table.

"Tristan," Les scratched his forehead, "could you get us some coffee, please?"

"Sure. What would you like in them?"

"Two sugar and no anchovies." She grinned as Tristan slumped against the door.

"Anchovies?" Les frowned.

"Tristan will tell you all about it," she said, and stood up, "since I've got lots to do." Isobel patted Tristan's shoulder. "Don't give the old man a hard time."

Les stared at the green and mauve veins covering his hands. He couldn't remember when the liver spots first appeared but the patches seemed to grow larger every month. He looked at Tristan and decided he didn't want to hear anything about anchovies.

"I trust you've made sure the working papers are clean and have followed all procedures correctly." He opened a file.

"Sure. As you can see, everything's well diarized. If it hadn't been for the bookkeeper I wouldn't have spotted the fraud as fast as I did."

After examining the files, Les had reached the same conclusion. "This bookkeeper sounds remarkably cooperative."

"God, yes. What a woman!" Tristan spotted Les's grim expression. "She was really helpful."

"And?"

"I asked her out. Thought maybe I could get more information on Roche."

"Have you gone on your date yet?"

"No."

"Break it."

Tristan was stunned. He'd never broken a date before. A man didn't do that to a lady, especially if she was a good-looking bookkeeper.

"This certainly is a sign of the times, isn't it?" He shook his head. "Broken dates, lousy managerial decisions, and white collar crime. The only good thing about a recession is that the lousy businessmen finally go under."

"Tristan," Les said coldly, "explain your procedures at Ice Craft."

He launched into a lengthy explanation, giving modest credit to Alex Bellamy's and Andy Gowan's part in the investigation.

"I'm glad you're so competent, Mr. Wells. Otherwise, you'd be out of a job, which would mean learning what a recession is all about."

Les closed the file as he looked at Tristan. "If you insist on becoming an accountant, then you'll have to learn that what you find isn't nearly as important as what you've missed, and what you've achieved isn't as important as what you could lose if you believe in your own asinine theories, which I doubt."

Tristan started to speak but Les cut him off. "I want you to go over the working papers to find all the things I know you've missed."

"It'll take time."

"You're competent, aren't you?"

Tristan's smile faded.

"Get Alfred's personal tax file from Jerry, would you, and ask him to join us." Les flipped through another file.

Tristan left the room, happy to be in on the secrets and scandals the fraud had exposed. Neither he nor his father had ever dreamed he'd find adventure in accounting, but over these past few weeks Tristan had discovered a whole range of possibilities. Business magazines were portraying accountants as the latest group of sexy, well-off professionals, and Tristan proudly identified with the image. Although acquiring the skills was a bit tricky, he was managing to cover his aspiring accountant's ass with every resource available.

As he approached Jerry's office, Jerry emerged with Marlena, and Tristan fell in love all over again. It happened every time he saw the lady, and once or twice she'd even winked at him.

"Jerry, Les wants to see you, and he asked that you bring Alfred Lin's personal tax file." He grinned at Marlena. "How are you, Mrs. Margolin?"

"Good, thanks." She spotted Craig and Martin hurrying

past her. "Mr. Sloane, Mr. McBride."

They greeted Marlena pensively and kept going. As Isobel walked past the group, Tristan noticed how she and Marlena barely glanced at one another. It was probably a competitive thing. Both women were strong and beautiful: queen bees at their respective offices.

"Darling, I'll see you later." Marlena kissed Jerry's cheek. "I'm glad one of your crises is over."

She smiled at Tristan. "Nice to see you again."

"I'm always here," he announced, "working hard for your husband."

"Lucky you." She winked at Jerry, then left.

Tristan followed Jerry into Les's office.

"Les, where is Jillian exactly?" Jerry asked.

"On a short vacation."

"If she calls I'd like to talk to her, see how she is."

Les opened the file Tristan handed him. "How's Alfred's personal tax situation?"

"I'm not sure. We haven't talked in a while."

"And Tony's?"

"Also up in the air. He was supposed to have brought in some receipts and information last Thursday night, but it didn't happen." Jerry sat in the chair opposite Les. "However, a situation has come up." He glanced at Tristan.

"Tristan," Les said, "I'm still waiting for my coffee."

He sprang out of his chair. "I'll be right back."

When the door was shut, Jerry explained Tony's proposal to invest in Ice Craft.

"He wants to know if Alfred will consider the idea," Jerry spoke softly. "It could solve his financial problems."

Not to mention Barker's legal concerns, Les thought. A partnership with Alfred would make it nearly impossible for Barker to be held liable for the fraud.

"Alfred won't go for it."

"Could you at least ask him?"

"I don't think he's in the mood for making deals these

days."

"I appreciate that; but he needs cash and, realistically, what are his chances with the banks?"

"I'll talk to him." Les tapped his pen on a note pad. "I found the Lions Imports file last night." He peered at Jerry. "The financial statements and corporate returns are missing. Have they shown up in your area yet?"

"I've just got his personal tax file."

"Terrific."

Tristan brought in the coffee, slopping some of it on the carpet.

"Tristan!"

"Sorry, but I'm no good at Jillian's job. How is she anyway? I heard she's pregnant."

"She's not pregnant!"

"Mononucleosis then? Hepatitis?"

"It's the bloody flu, and why are you so interested?"

"Because I miss her," he answered cheerfully. "Don't you?"

FIFTEEN

In Chinatown, Kelly Faust walked down East Pender Street and tried not to inhale the smell of barbecued ducks hanging in restaurants' and butchers' windows. His stomach couldn't take it this morning.

After an all-night vigil, he'd seen Alex emerge from an alley at the southwest corner of Main and Hastings early this morning. He followed him now, keeping to the other side of the street. A blue Oldsmobile also tailed Alex. Its driver was an acquaintance of Faust's; someone he'd hired after his Silby & Morrow contact had refused to go near the area.

It was hard to keep up with Alex in the crowd. Shoppers hovered around the sidewalk's fruit and vegetable displays. People chatted in the middle of the sidewalk while others waited near the curb and tried to stay out of the way. Several times Faust bumped into youngsters or their mothers whose grim, exhausted faces reminded him of his own mom.

When he was four years old, his father had picked him up, held him before his sobbing mother and ordered him to hit her. The bastard shook him until his arms and legs were forced to swing at her. Once, when his mother was half out of her mind and close to a complete breakdown, she had tried to poison his father. He was seven years old when she left.

Faust used to spend countless hours wondering where

she'd gone. The day he was strong enough to fight back, he stopped wondering about her altogether. At age fifteen, Faust left his father writhing on the kitchen floor, semi-crippled and helpless while he walked out, not expecting to hear from the old man again.

Three years later, a colleague of his father spotted Faust panhandling on East Hastings Street. Tired of begging, Faust had accepted the man's offer of work in Revenue Canada's mail room, provided his father wasn't told about his employment. It took a while to learn of the colleague's betrayal. It took many more years to learn about his father's letter in his personnel file. To this day, Victor Faust wasn't an easy memory to kill. His photograph was a caustic reminder that although he'd passed on he hadn't really died, not the way Kelly wanted him to be dead. . . . almost, but not yet.

♦ ♦ ♦

Alex hurried out of the bakery carrying breakfast for Jillian, and continued down East Pender thinking again about the events of the night before. Les's phone call was followed by another call from Tristan, who provided a firsthand account of the altercation in the stairwell. He told Alex about a short man in a black raincoat with light coloured hair and a blue and red face mask in his hand. Aware of what the mask had meant to Alex, Tristan had promptly shoved the door in the guy's face. Alex pictured the mask and the razor blade slashing his cheek with two swift strokes. He glanced at the pedestrians around him and trembled as the cool April breeze penetrated his clothes.

His assailant could have been the Special Investigations contact. Tristan knew what Sam Roche, Tony Barker, and Alfred Lin looked like, but last night's visitor was a new face. The partner involved in the fraud must have listened to their phone conversation, then perhaps instructed the contact to meet him there. Tristan believed the file had been placed in the file room simply to see who would take it.

Faces peered at Alex through bus and shop windows. Cars

crawled by. He listened to footsteps behind him, and focused on the entrance to the alley ahead. He hoped Jillian would be helpful this morning. Late last night, he'd asked her to recall the names of any Revenue Canada people who'd been in contact with the firm, but she said it was hard enough remembering clients, let alone tax officials. If he could show her a list of Special Investigations personnel, though, she might recognize a name. It'd be simpler to identify one person than rehash every partner's activities over recent weeks. As Alex wondered how he'd obtain a personnel list, he turned the corner and spotted Jillian standing in the middle of the alley. She was gazing at the buildings on either side of her.

"You forgot to lock the door," she said as he slowly approached.

"Didn't think I needed to."

"I'd decided to join you, but by the time I got outside you'd disappeared so I thought I'd wait here." Jillian glanced at Carnegie Centre. "I wasn't sure I could find my way back through the tunnel."

A blue Oldsmobile crawled up the alley towards Alex. Alex turned around. A blue Oldsmobile had been parked next to the alley on Hastings Street when he'd stepped out of the cellar. He'd seen it again after leaving the alley and turning onto Pender Street.

The car stopped ten yards in front of them. The driver was alone, opening his door, and pointing a gun at Alex.

Alex pulled and aimed his own weapon. They both fired. The man's gun fell on the ground. His hand drained blood onto the ground and left a trail that followed him inside the car.

Alex grabbed Jillian's hand and started to run. The vehicle roared forward. He shot at the windshield, then fired again, but the car kept coming.

He yanked Jillian out of the way, throwing her off balance. She fell against a dumpster as the car raced out of the alley.

He helped her up. "Are you all right?"

She winced with pain. "I've hurt my arm."

After checking her over he said, "I don't think anything's broken. Let's go downstairs."

Alex secured the cellar door behind them, then picked up his flashlight and the lantern he'd left with Jillian. He opened a trap door in the floor.

"I'll go first, then help you down the ladder."

Before he touched the ground, she started after him.

"Close the door above you."

As she reached for the handle her foot slipped, thumping Alex in the chest. He lost his grip, swayed backward, then grabbed a rung.

The tunnel at this end was mucky. Puddles of water stank of decaying rodents and garbage. Old Coke bottles and tin cans were partially submerged in the muck. With his arm around her waist, Alex stumbled down the tunnel, stopping every few seconds to look behind him.

When they reached Jillian's room, he collapsed beside her on the cot. Sweat trickled down his back. Alex removed his glasses and rubbed the bridge of his nose. He wiped his mouth with the back of his hand as the razor cuts on his cheek throbbed.

"Jillian, are you okay?"

She gripped the edge of the cot until her knuckles turned white.

"Jillian?" He put his glasses back on, then gazed at her long, outstretched legs and the black blouse partially hidden under her cardigan. Carefully, he swept dark strands of hair out of her eyes.

Suddenly she sneezed, then sneezed again.

"I've arranged to move you to a warm, safe place. It'll be great."

Jillian glared at him as she searched her left sleeve for a tissue. "I told you, I hate guns."

"I had to protect you. You came that close to getting shot!"

Alex's hand shook as he showed her the tiny space between

his thumb and finger.

"Wrong." She rubbed her feet together to extract the mud from her white runners. "You're the one who came close to getting shot. The gun was aimed at you."

"And after he shot me he would have gone for you."

"You don't know that."

"Yes, I do."

"No, you don't."

"Yes, I—"

"No!"

"Why would he leave an eyewitness to my murder?"

She stared at her running shoes.

"Anyway, you don't have to worry. I've had training with firearms."

"Revenue Canada was giving a seminar, was it?" She sneezed again.

"My dad loves guns. He sent this one to me; insisted I learn how to use it."

Jillian searched the right sleeve of her cardigan, and removed a tissue.

"It's a pistol: a Smith & Wesson 469 mini-gun," he continued, "with a safety—"

"Could we talk about something else?" Jillian blew her nose, then shoved the tissue in her pocket.

"You're not getting sick on me, are you?"

"Allergies. I'm probably allergic to mould and decay on top of everything else. Maybe I'm allergic to you."

"Tell me what you need and I'll get it from the drug store."

"I'd appreciate that, thanks."

"No problem."

She stared at him for several seconds. "Who was the guy in the alley?"

"Don't know. I take it you've never seen him until today?"

"No."

"He must be connected to the fraud."

Jillian studied Alex's eyes. One was a slightly lighter shade of blue than the other, but she couldn't tell if this was natural or whether the cuts and bruises on his face were creating this effect.

He said, "Do you know which partner prepared financial statements for Lions Imports last year?"

She shook her head.

"Who else, except a partner, could falsify Lions Imports financial statements and get away with it?"

"What?"

"Copies from your and Tony Barker's offices, not to mention the originals from our office, are missing. I think a partner wants to hide the fact that something's wrong with the numbers."

"Alex, they're C.A.s, for God's sake, not criminals. Sometimes they're jerks and once in awhile somebody says something malicious, but accountants aren't financial risk-takers by nature. None of them would jeopardize their careers to get involved with Barker, or Sam Roche."

As Jillian picked at a tissue she remembered Les asking her to arrange an appointment with his lawyer. "If you're right about the statements, then sooner or later someone will notice the numbers. I just can't picture our partners setting themselves up for that kind of trouble."

"Suppose someone in Special Investigations already knows about the statements and is protecting the partner? It could explain the arrangements Roche alluded to." Alex observed her skeptical gaze. "Have any of them had recent contact with Roche, Barker, or someone from S.I.?"

Jillian thought of Jerry's friendship with Barker. As a tax partner, he'd also have regular contact with Revenue Canada on behalf of various clients. Her light green eyes stared at Alex suspiciously.

"You don't think a partner had something to do with your friend's murder, do you?"

Alex flopped on his side and gazed at a wall. "Maybe we

should find out why you're so protective of your bosses. Are you hiding something, or are you worried about losing your job?"

"I don't know what to think these days. Things have gone from bad to worse since the phone calls started."

Alex sat up. "You said you've been getting phone calls for a week?"

"They started after I got home late from work Thursday night."

"When did you start losing things at the office?"

"The next day."

Alex's thigh nudged hers as he clasped his hands together. "Did anything unusual happen that Thursday?"

"Alex, I don't think this will help you. It's pretty boring stuff."

"Okay, tell me about your family instead."

She stared at him. "What for?"

"Because I'd like to talk about something that won't make you so tense."

"How do you know that talking about my family won't make me more tense?"

He paused. "Oh."

"So, what would you like to know?"

"Do you have any brothers or sisters?"

"I'm an only child."

"What do your parents do?"

She stood up. "My mother's agoraphobic. My father retired early to stay with her because she can't cope on her own. I really would like to call her soon, if that's okay."

"You can use the phone at our new place."

Jillian strolled around the room. "Tell me about your parents."

Alex looked at the lime green turtle on top of Jillian's clothes bag. "They're outgoing, social people; comfortably well off and semi-retired from the hospitality industry."

Jillian fumbled with her sleeves. "That's weird. I thought

I had more than one tissue tucked away."

"Your pockets bulge with them."

"Those are used ones. I keep unused ones up my sleeve and used ones in my pockets."

"How organized of you."

Jillian tried to turn the sleeves inside out. "Alex, I think I've dropped some tissues in the tunnel." She gazed at him. "I know I had more than these on me."

He sprang off the cot. "I hope you haven't left a trail."

As he pressed his ear to the door Jillian looked at his damp bangs. She liked Alex in a sweat, all anxious and human: almost sexy.

"What is it?"

"Shhh."

As she put her hand on his shoulder, Alex slipped an arm around her.

"We're leaving," he murmured.

"Now?"

He looked at her. "Scared?"

"I'm not cut out for this kind of adventure, Alex."

"That's too bad because I think we have company."

Jillian leaned against the door, then heard the sound of paper rustling. "Oh no!"

"Get your stuff." He slipped his gun out of his waistband.

She grabbed her purse and paper bag. "Shouldn't we play this a little more cautiously?"

"Who knows?"

Alex closed his eyes and whispered a prayer. He then flung the door open and jumped into the hallway with both hands gripping the pistol. No one was there, except for seven large rats devouring the remnants of last night's sandwiches. He sprang back and slammed the door behind him.

"Oh God!"

"What is it?"

"Rats in the hallway! Eating scraps of last night's sandwiches. I knew I should have done a better job of cleaning up."

Jillian folded her arms. "Isn't this typical? Other women get James Bond and I get a Revenue Canada auditor terrified of rodents."

Alex slowly opened the door. "Eeuuu."

"Want me to hold your hand?"

"I can manage, thanks."

Alex led Jillian through the black musty silence towards the alley. Swiftly he climbed the ladder, opened the trap door and entered the cellar. As Alex helped Jillian up, the light from a crack in the outer door disappeared. Suddenly some-one kicked the door.

Horror wrapped itself around Alex's neck and pulled tight. He pictured Andy's body, and glowering blue-grey eyes in the parking lot. He visualized the car in the alley: pedestrians watching. A short man with a patched eye and a black raincoat had stood at the end of the alley. He'd been particularly interested.

"Downstairs, quick!"

As Jillian descended the ladder someone smashed against the door, then kicked it again.

"Go!" Alex clambered down the ladder after her. As she reached the ground, he tripped and fell, dropping the lantern. "Shit!"

His left leg was hooked on a rung. His right leg and arm sank in the muck as he tried to get up. The cellar door started to give way.

Jillian dropped her shopping bag, then freed Alex's leg.

"We'll have to leave through the Centre!" he yelled.

Alex grabbed the lantern as Jillian lifted her bag. Smelly muck on the bottom of it plopped onto her clothes.

They hurried back down the tunnel, taking the route that veered to the left. Alex opened the small door on the right.

"If you spot the guy in the Oldsmobile, or a short man in a black raincoat, holler."

"What short man?"

"I'll tell you later."

In the office adjoining the storage room, a steaming cup of coffee and a freshly lit cigarette sat on a desk. In the room beyond, people browsed through newspapers and magazines while others played card games.

Taking Jillian's hand, Alex strolled into the reception area while people stared at their muddy clothes, the dented lantern, and the cuts on his face. He stopped at the exit.

"Ready, Jillian?"

"No. I hate this."

Peering through the doors, Alex saw two ancient, grungy-looking men kneeling on the stairs. The man on the left gaped at him with a brown toothless mouth. The second man picked a cigarette butt off the step. Below them several rough-looking types lounged on the stairs.

There was no sign of the Oldsmobile or anyone in a black raincoat. Alex and Jillian stepped outside and surveyed the congested Main and Hastings intersection. While they waited for the stoplight to change to green, Jillian inhaled the smell of urine and unwashed bodies. A few pedestrians at the stoplight wore suits but most sported jeans and long greasy hair. A couple of men were drunk. One woman sat propped against the building, asleep. Jillian stepped closer to Alex and took his hand.

"Nervous?" he asked.

"I don't feel safe around here. Two months ago, my friend was waiting for the traffic light to change when some guy opened the passenger door where her five-year-old was sitting, and demanded money."

As they dodged across the intersection, a car swiftly turned in front of them, nearly hitting Alex. They started to run. Jillian glanced behind her and saw a blur of people. For a moment, she thought she saw someone in black watching them from the top step of the Carnegie Centre.

SIXTEEN

"Connie, I want you to revise this letter." Martin Sloane placed a sheet of paper on top of the receptionist's switchboard. "My secretary typed B.C. instead of British Columbia, and the additions need checking."

"I'm a little busy right now. Can it wait until she's back from lunch?"

"Connie," Tristan said and waved some papers at her, "the photocopier needs some pooper in it. These copies are too light."

"Tristan!" Les marched towards him. "Why are you asking our receptionist to fix the photocopier?"

"Because everyone else is at lunch."

"Partners' work takes priority," Martin snapped. "Honest to God, Leslie, this situation's ridiculous. We don't have enough typists and my work isn't getting done!"

"Have you tried patience? It works wonders."

Martin stormed off as Les scowled at Tristan until he got the message and also left.

"Connie, I'm sorry," he said, "but Jillian will be back soon."

"Don't worry about it. I can handle them."

"Would you please tell Jerry that Alfred Lin called to confirm tomorrow's meeting with Mr. Barker?" He looked up to see Isobel Cameron walking towards him. "Isobel, do you know if Tony Barker had been in contact with anyone from Revenue Canada before the Ice Craft matter occurred?"

"I have no idea." Isobel picked up her phone messages. She was sorting through them when Craig called Connie's name. As he strolled towards the group, a missing shirt button exposed black hairs on his oversized stomach.

"I thought you'd gone home," Les remarked.

"Change of plans." He leaned close to Connie. "Are you free for lunch?"

Craig knew his lunches with the clerical staff irritated his partners. Most of the women couldn't keep their mouths shut, and Craig had become an expert at friendly interrogation. He'd learned a few things about his colleagues this way and had grown especially fond of dangling bits of gossip in front of Martin.

"Not today, thanks," Connie answered.

Craig stared at Isobel. "You want to eat with me?"

"No."

He watched her for several seconds. "I bet you have amazingly low heating bills."

"You can bet all you like," she retorted, as she watched him turn his back to her and stroll away, "but you'll never know."

Isobel ignored Les's puzzled expression as she repinned a loose strand of dark blonde hair. He was about to say something when Jerry approached.

"Jerry, do you know if Tony spoke to any Revenue Canada people before the auditors appeared on his doorstep?" Les asked.

"He's always receiving their love letters. Why?"

"From the same person?"

"From different people," Jerry replied. "Tony wants to see Ice Craft's statements for the last three years before tomorrow's meeting. Can we arrange that?"

"You're meeting Barker tomorrow?" Isobel asked.

Les briefly explained the man's proposal to invest a million dollars for the privilege of co-owning Ice Craft

Jewellers, then added nothing was likely to come of it. Alfred Lin hated the idea of sitting down with Sam Roche, but Les wanted Roche there. The company's financial crisis would be discussed. It would then be made clear that, if Roche wanted to avoid a police investigation, and Barker wanted to invest in Ice Craft, then Roche would first have to name his accomplice in the fraud.

"Aren't you asking for trouble with Roche and Alfred in the same room?" Jerry asked.

"I'll deal with Alfred."

"Considering the situation with Ice Craft and Lions Imports," Isobel said, "shouldn't the partners have been told about the meeting?"

"Considering the way Lions files have been mishandled, I didn't think the partners would be interested in Mr. Barker's latest venture."

"Craig would," she smiled coolly, "unless he's found another file to sabotage."

"Isobel, may I have a private word with you?"

Les walked towards the chairs in a corner of the lobby. She followed slowly while continuing to read phone messages.

He glanced at the worn brown carpet and beige walls and reminded himself to re-do the lobby when order was restored. The colours had been John's idea of respectability; they reminded Les of a shabby dental office.

He folded his arms as she stopped in front of him. "I don't appreciate that kind of talk in front of the staff."

"Wake up, Les," she whispered. "Everyone knows about Craig's so-called incompetency with files, especially the ones I've worked on."

"I thought we agreed that any number changes were due to careless, inexperienced students."

"We agreed on nothing. The numbers may have stopped changing, but repercussions are still surfacing and it makes me look bad. Lions Imports is just one example."

Les looked doubtful, uneasy.

"No wonder he keeps late hours," she murmured. "It must take a lot of work to change whole sets of statements, unless he has Martin's help, which wouldn't surprise me." She started to turn away, then stopped. "Do you think Martin will ever forgive us for my becoming partner, or must we put up with the bad-mouthing and accusations until he drops dead at his desk? Now, if you'll excuse me, I have to fax something to a client."

Les followed her out of the lobby, then walked down the hall in the opposite direction. After last night's incident in the stairwell, he realized that whatever small hope he'd held onto of the firm's blamelessness in the Ice Craft fraud was gone. Alex's suspicions about a partner's guilt in the fraud worried him. He had planned to establish the firm's innocence, then form a committee to fight the slackening distinction between right and wrong in this office; however, now that he really needed Isobel's and Jerry's support, both seemed ready to turn their backs on him.

Les knocked on Craig's door. When there was no answer, he opened the door and stepped into a room where memos covered the walls at all angles. Scribbled notes were taped over Craig's diploma and the room stank of old smoke.

Les opened a drawer in search of a cigarette. He'd smoked three in the last six years: one after John Morrow's death, the second after his divorce, the third after Jerry's wedding. He was ready for a fourth.

In the second drawer, Les found a handful of coasters with female names scrawled across them. A date was scribbled under each name. Some coasters were months old, others more recent. Matchbooks and hotel receipts had been paper clipped together. The top receipt came from the Skylark Hotel and was dated April 2nd: today's date.

Les had once had a client who'd conducted all of his meetings at the Skylark: a narrow, grimy little place with young-looking strippers and a crude clientele. Worse still, the hotel was near Main and Hastings Streets, the area where Alex had demanded that the money be dropped. Every partner had heard him name the location at the last meeting. Judging from these receipts, the hotel was often frequented by Craig.

Craig appeared in the doorway. He entered the room and saw the receipts in Les's hand.

"What were you doing at the Skylark this morning?" Les tossed the receipts on the desk.

Craig shut the door. "None of your business."

"The Skylark Hotel is close to my business! What the hell have you done?"

He looked at the open drawers. "Leslie, I don't want anyone going through my desk when I'm not here. You, of all people, should respect my privacy."

"You shouldn't have been anywhere near that area when Jillian's safety was at stake!"

"She's safe now, isn't she? So don't worry about it. Maybe I should have stayed at a higher-priced hotel, but the truth is my wife kicked me out a couple of days ago and I can't afford better."

Les stared at him. "Is Liz all right?"

"She's doing great without me." He nodded at the open drawers. "You might as well continue snooping; you're almost done anyway," Craig added, then smiled. "Don't forget to search Martin's office, too. The Skylark, as you probably don't know, has a good view of the police station, and who do you think I saw coming out of there about seven-thirty this morning?"

There was a brief knock at the door and Martin walked in.

"Speak of the devil. Still following me, old man?" Craig removed a pack of cigarettes from the bottom drawer. "Forgot these."

He started to leave, then stopped. "Feel free to help Les go through the crap, Martin, although I don't think anything's changed since your last visit. You should take the T1 file though, since there's only twenty-eight days to complete the three hundred and ten income tax returns listed inside."

"We were supposed to go over this weeks ago!" Martin shouted.

Assigning Craig's T1 responsibilities to Martin had created one more contentious issue between them; but Les didn't think there would have been a need to intervene if Craig had done a good job last year. If both men behaved maturely then the transfer wouldn't be a problem now.

"Do either of you know if Barker had dealings with Revenue Canada before the audit?"

"Why ask me?" Martin retorted. "I've had nothing to do with the client."

"Isobel knows," Craig muttered as he slipped the cigarettes in his pocket, "and if she denies it she's lying."

Les stared at him. "She's not the only liar around here."

"Indeed." Martin turned to Les. "I've come to tell you that Sam Roche is on the phone. Apparently, he wants to talk about tomorrow's meeting with Barker and Alfred Lin."

Craig lit a cigarette. "Taking things into your own hands again, Les?"

"Somebody has to."

"Enjoy." Craig shut the door behind him.

Les looked at Martin. "Do you have any lunch plans?"

"I'm meeting Jerry."

"Then I'll join you."

"I wish you wouldn't." He left the room.

Les tossed the receipts in the drawer and stared out the window as the telephone rang. He didn't want to talk to Roche when it seemed more urgent to search each partner's office and find out what else was being kept from him.

The unanswered call transferred itself back to Connie Sekata's switchboard. While she spoke to Roche, a local lit up the board as a partner dialled Kelly Faust's phone number.

SEVENTEEN

Jerry Margolin drove up to a house on Third Avenue in New Westminster. The building was a disjointed mausoleum piece bought by Tony and painted pale green. Tony had turned it into a restaurant because he knew old houses aroused curiosity, particularly when they housed the chance of a good meal inside. Jerry walked through the dining room between a variety of colourful table settings and large, comfortable-looking chairs. He found Tony in the kitchen stirring a pot of what smelled like sweet oranges.

"Jerry!" Tony waved him over. "Come taste my Grand Marnier soup."

Tony's face was hot and shiny, his sleeves rolled up to expose large, almost hairless forearms. "Did you bring the financial statements?"

"Yes."

While Jerry tried the soup, he watched Tony study an Ice Craft statement with the care and attention of someone who enjoyed reading balance sheets. He knew Tony had once been a controller, then later a purchasing agent. In these positions, he'd successfully invested his money in stocks and real estate, although to what extent Jerry was no longer sure. His financial picture had grown ambiguous in recent months, and at times Tony was disturbingly uncooperative about releasing information.

After the job offer, Jerry grew reluctant about socializing

with Tony. He didn't want to discover that the purchasing agent turned entrepreneur had particular legal reasons for keeping financial secrets. He didn't want to know anything about those secrets, in case ties had to be quickly severed.

"You said normalized maintainable earnings were about one and a half million." Tony looked up from the statements. "In what shape are this year's receivables?"

"Les will be bringing the current year's statements, but I gather they're up twenty or thirty percent from last year. This soup is very good."

"Thank you. My wife pinched the recipe from a chef in Paris." Tony watched him closely. "Tell me, what are my chances of getting a fifty-one percent interest in the com-company?"

"I doubt if the shareholders would go for it."

"You said his father-in-law and uncles own fifteen common shares each?"

Jerry nodded.

"What if I offered to buy whatever they were willing to sell?"

"They're Chinese businessmen, and not likely to let a white person get controlling interest in the family business."

"I could offer them three and three-quarter million dollars altogether, more than enough to start a new business."

The front door slammed and Sam Roche shouted hello.

"So," Tony said and closed the financial statements, "the shows begins. Bring your things in the dining room, and don't look so worried."

As Jerry chose a seat next to the window, it started to rain. He felt unprepared for this meeting. After the discussion with Tony last Thursday night, he'd placed his personal income tax file back in the cabinet; now it was gone. Roche, Alfred Lin, and Les Silby's arrival filled the room with tension. Les looked tired and subdued, while Alfred scowled and Roche grinned idiotically.

"Jerry!" Sam acted surprised to see him. "God, it must

be eight months since I've seen you."

"Yes." Jerry's smile was strained. "How are you?"

"Still a bachelor. Congratulations on your marriage. Your wife's an exotic-looking lady, really something."

Jerry saw Roche look at Alfred and sensed Alfred's hostility deepening. He felt his own embarrassment develop inexplicably and wished he was with Marlena now.

Tony carried in a tray with five bowls of soup. "A small treat, gentlemen, before we begin."

Sam peered in his bowl. "Carrot soup?"

"Just try it, Sam."

Tony served himself the smallest portion, ate quickly, and asked to see Ice Craft's current financial statements. Alfred Lin nodded to Les, who promptly handed Tony the sheets. The room was silent until he'd finished scanning the first three pages.

"You did very well last year, Alfred."

"My designers are excellent," he answered bluntly. "Very loyal employees."

"You see no further cash flow problems this year?"

Jerry held his breath and wondered why Tony was playing games with the man. He saw the hostility deepen in Alfred's eyes. Jerry had seen Alfred deal with people he didn't like and was afraid he'd grow loud and nasty.

"No, I do not see further cash problems."

Tony paused and nodded slowly. "Jerry came up with a plan where Ice Craft would issue a thousand preferred shares which I'd purchase for one million dollars in cash. This would just be the initial investment, you understand. Further payment would come after conversion to common shares."

Alfred stared at him.

"Jerry," Tony turned to him, "can you give us an idea of the tax consequences of this plan?"

He hesitated. "It would depend on the circumstances surrounding your personal tax positions, but generally speaking a feasible arrangement could be positive, provided it's completed properly and within an appropriate time frame."

Tony smiled. He always enjoyed the way Jerry made uncertainty sound like a hundred-dollar opinion. He turned to Alfred.

"Naturally, this arrangement would be strictly between us, nor do I wish to interfere with the company's operation in any way."

"Wait." Sam dropped his spoon in the soup bowl. "I think Tony's forgot something here."

Tony stared at him. "Have I, Mr. Roche?"

"You and I talked about my investing in Ice Craft, remember?"

Alfred started to speak, but Les touched his shoulder. He wanted to hear more about his talk with Barker.

"I don't recall the conversation," Tony frowned slightly, "and I really don't see how a partnership between us is possible."

Sam lit a cigarette and smiled at the challenge in Tony's eyes.

"You're right, my mistake. I intended to call you about it, but I've been spending a lot of time up the coast near Sechelt."

Tony didn't move. Jerry glanced at Les who was listening carefully.

"Just off the coast, about a ten-minute drive beyond the City's centre, are a few privately owned islands, some of them only a few hundred yards from shore." Sam rubbed his chin and smiled at the intensity of Tony's gaze. "One of them has a mansion. From what I've seen and heard, it's quite the spot."

Tony stood up and walked to the kitchen, returning a moment later with five glasses and a bottle of Scotch. When everyone had been served, he raised his glass.

"Gentlemen, a toast."

Glasses were lifted cautiously.

"To free enterprise and to Revenue Canada, which works so hard to keep us honest."

Les nearly dropped his glass.

"To the taxpayers," Sam said. "The t.p.s, which also stands for toilet paper and we know what Revenue Canada does with its toilet paper."

"Roche, shut up." Alfred clutched his glass as if ready to chuck it at him.

"Relax Alfred, you're always so tense." His hand gently touched his bruised rib cage. "Let's drink to Jerry's new wife, Marlena. You have met her, haven't you, Alfred?" He winked at his ex-boss's frozen expression.

As Jerry drank, he recalled Marlena's reference to a business on Tony's island. He remembered Tony's own description of the property, accompanied by written details and a plastic card to gain admittance to the estate; the place where Jerry was to have joined him and Marlena last weekend before work deadlines changed his plans.

The route Tony had drawn for him that Thursday night matched the location Roche just described. When Les walked in on their meeting, Tony had plunked the Scotch bottle over the map in a sloppy attempt to hide it. The next day, Les had been disgusted as he lifted the bottle high enough to expose the sticky scrap of paper underneath. He'd lectured him about controlling messy clients. He hadn't commented on the map itself, but he'd seen it.

The island was one more mysterious and unwelcome aspect of Tony: the ubiquitous force in a tug of war between what was secretive and what was intimate. He couldn't possibly go there now, and for one brief moment Jerry was relieved, until he saw the accusation in the look Les gave him.

EIGHTEEN

Sam Roche lived on a secluded piece of property in West Vancouver. He rented the house from an architect friend who'd paid two million dollars to build a life removed from neighbours and kids selling raffle tickets. By the time the architect was due to return from his year-long trek through the Australian outback, Sam figured he'd be able to afford his own fancy home. He looked out at the cars crowding his driveway. After spreading rumours about his pending wealth, he found that everyone wanted his company.

Sam was pleased with the way he'd dropped just enough hints at the Sapphire Club to arouse Tony's curiosity, and with the way he'd supplied further detail about the island at this morning's meeting. If Tony wanted to keep his island a secret, then he'd have to pay for the privilege. Sam had won and here he was, ready and waiting on a gold-plated roof one floor below heaven. Heaven was spicy — his fingertips touched it and brushed against the odds of coming this far in such a short time.

Tony should have phoned by now to offer some payment to his old buddy Sam. Taking an address book from his pocket, Sam dialled the Sapphire Club's number and was told he'd be contacted shortly. One minute later the telephone rang.

"Mr. Roach?"

"Marlena, is that you, darling?" He tossed the address

book on his bed. "You sound like you're talking in a tin can."

"A Jaguar, actually. Are you at home?"

"Yeah. You should see my place some time. Course, the hiding spots aren't as comfy as the ones on Alfred's property, but I could show you just as many interesting poses."

There was no response.

"I want to talk to Tony," he added.

"He's not available."

"Is that right? Well, tell the old bastard I hope he doesn't take me for a fool because—"

"Mr. Roach, he can't take what's being given away." She hung up.

Sam slammed the receiver down. He picked up the phone, threw it on the floor, then used the receiver to smash the dial. He threw the phone again as a female voice crooned, "Poor Sammy."

Two women stood in the doorway, similarly shaped and dressed in identical blue underpants. They sat down on the floor and smiled sly, glazed smiles.

"You're missing the party, Sam."

They unbuttoned his shirt, then slowly unzipped his trousers. Sam slipped his hands under their silk and pinched with all of his strength. He pretended they were identical Marlena sluts, slippery and soft and submissive. His own passion was black and oily, like a cold cup of coffee choked with grounds. He prodded, attacked, and bubbled, then collapsed on the carpet while the women stood up and re-joined the party.

Sam stumbled after them into a large darkened room where bodies grovelled over one another like rodents. Furniture had been pushed against the wall. Drinks were spilled and clothing scattered as the bodies became entangled and rhythmic and sweaty. The music blared and lungs burst; mouths opened, groaned, and clamped onto flesh.

The weeds, mushrooms, and powders in Sam's special

bowls were almost gone. He carried the bowls through the kitchen, then onto the porch outside. Sam hurried down the steps, stopping midway as something moved in the shadows. He squinted into the darkness. "Hello?"

Someone stepped forward, then stopped.

Sam gripped the rail and leaned forward. "Is that a cop in my bushes?"

The man stepped into view.

"Alfred!"

Alfred Lin glanced at Sam's greenish naked body, then looked away in disgust. "I want your photographs."

"Remember the island I mentioned this morning?" Shivering, Sam put the bowls on a table and folded his arms. "Marlena goes there a lot with Tony, and guess how she entertains herself when hubby's not around? You're not her only lover, you know."

Alfred's eyes were murderous.

"I think Tony wants all of Ice Craft," Sam walked down the steps, "but I've got enough on him to make sure you aren't double-crossed."

"Stay out of my life!"

Sam stood in front of Alfred, too stoned, confident, and cold to think clearly.

"Don't tell me you've fallen for that whore. Oh boy, Alf—"

Alfred swung his fist but Sam ducked, then lost his balance and fell. As Alfred approached him, Sam scrambled backwards up the steps.

"She has the photos you've taken, right Alfred? How much would you lose if your family saw them, and what would Marlena do with the pictures if you crossed her?"

"I want your pictures plus the negatives now!"

"Okay fine, just relax."

Alfred waited at the bottom of the stairs while Sam entered the house, limping slightly. In the bedroom he removed an envelope from a drawer, pulled out his favourite snapshot of Marlena, then tossed the envelope on the bed.

In the bathroom, he bent over the sink and splashed his face with water while the door opened, then softly closed. When Sam looked up, an unexpected visitor stood three feet behind him. He turned around, then started to laugh.

"Well, well . . . I suppose I shouldn't be surprised. I knew you'd want to see me sooner or later."

A smile slid over the visitor's lips. "You had no business at the meeting today."

The visitor held Sam's photographs and address book in hands protected by brown leather gloves. The book was turned to the page with Tony's name written above a route to the island. Notes and a detailed sketch of the property filled the opposite page.

"This little discovery isn't for your use either. What did you plan to do with this information?"

"Sell it to the highest bidder."

The visitor nodded. "You've been thorough about recording activities on the island."

"I managed to get inside the mansion; play a few games with some rather unusual twists. Thanks for letting me keep some of the gems, by the way. They came in handy. Would you like to know what else, and who else, I saw there, because I'd be happy to tell you, for a price."

"Not interested," the visitor answered. "In fact, nobody's interested in you anymore, Sam."

The photographs and book were pocketed away, then swiftly replaced with a needle.

"You've offended too many people."

Sam backed into the counter and then lunged for the door, but the visitor was quicker. Sam's forehead was slammed against the mirror. He watched the needle rise and puncture his arm. There was a flash of silver — a scream — liquid emptying into him. As Sam fell, the needle jumped from his arm. His fingertips touched it and brushed against the odds of coming this far in such a short time.

NINETEEN

Jillian stood in the middle of a plush, grey carpet in a living room accented with black furniture, a hi-tech entertainment centre, and colourful ornaments. This morning, she basked in the sunlight and fresh air of an apartment sixteen floors above street level, and was even trying a little exercise.

Hitching up her pyjama bottoms, she lifted her right leg, bending it at the knee. Jillian hugged the knee close to her chest as she watched the clown barbs and black mollies in Alex's fish tank. The fish swam close to the glass, turned sharply and glided across the tank. As Jillian drew her left knee up, the pyjama leg hung well below her foot.

"I wish you'd brought a nightgown when you raided my apartment, Alex. Your P.J.s are too big."

"Then don't wear them."

"Maybe I should call my mom back and have her send mine over."

He didn't respond.

"Thanks for letting me talk to her."

"Uh-huh."

Alex had been attentive and courteous all weekend, but seemed strangely moody this morning. He was kind of sexy, too, and more handsome every day as the bruises and cuts healed. She liked the way he wore his sensuality like an old wristwatch, hardly consulted but there all the same.

Once or twice she'd thought about trying to put this strange relationship on a more normal and intimate track, but she'd never learned how to show interest in a guy without feeling like a silly tramp.

Alex hadn't touched her once, nor had he talked about Andy; still, she was sure he thought of him. She'd seen the sadness in his face and regretted how difficult she'd been in the tunnel. She'd tried to compensate for her behaviour by offering to help with the cooking and housework; however, he'd insisted on doing everything. He'd barely sat still since they got here.

Alex marched across the living room wearing an apron designed like a tuxedo. A painted red bow tie sat under his chin and a white bib covered his chest. He hadn't shaved this morning, and his hair was a tangle of brown and gold. At the window, he squinted at the Beach Avenue traffic below, then marched back to the stove and flung paprika over scrambled eggs.

"I think you should exercise more often." Jillian sat on the floor. "It'd help you relax."

"If I exercised like you I'd fall asleep."

"These are legitimate warm-up exercises for ex-ballerinas," she replied.

"Is that the only exercising you do?"

"I walk a fair amount. Do you work out?"

"I ski and play racquet sports; do a little running. I like to keep active."

"So I've noticed."

Alex shook salt over the eggs. "How did you sleep?"

"I dreamed a lot."

"What about?"

"Nothing much."

He rolled sausages around in a second frying pan. "I think you spent the night trying to figure out which partner's involved in a fraud conspiracy with someone at Revenue Canada."

Jillian stood up and sauntered to the kitchen table. "Maybe you should concentrate on finding a co-conspirator in Special Investigations."

Alex popped two pieces of bread in the toaster. "I've tried."

He'd called the office three times to try to get a list of S.I. personnel, and to find out who'd been in charge over the last couple of weeks; however, anyone who knew him wanted to know why he hadn't come to work and why he wanted the information.

Sitting sideways in the chair, Jillian flexed her right foot and pointed it towards the floor.

"How did a nut like you wind up at Revenue Canada anyway?"

"I'm a C.A. with two years experience in industry." He slid a plate of sausages and eggs in front of her. "I like auditing and finding frauds, which is why I'm interested in your firm's partners."

Alex returned Jillian's glare because he knew the remark irritated her. He'd found that she didn't say anything useful when she was calm and friendly. He wanted her to blurt out everything she was keeping from him.

"I've heard a lot of talk," she replied as she shook her serviette open, "but you haven't given me any real evidence of fraud."

"Let me show you what I've got so far." Alex hurried out of the kitchen, and returned a minute later with a group of files.

"I wrote up a balance sheet for January and February." He handed the sheet to her. "Inventory valued at $25,162 represents all the jewellery, silver, and gold Ice Craft had at the end of February."

"So?"

"Look under accounts payable." He buttered the toast.

She looked further down the page, under the liabilities heading.

"I analyzed Ice Craft's payments during those months. They paid $160,268 in bills. $150,100 of it went to Lions Imports to buy gems," Alex said. "Turn to the income statement and look at the top line." He pointed at the number with his butter knife. "Sales were only $10,439 in those same two months, yet Ice Craft had little inventory to show for the purchases. So where did the stones go?"

"Are you sure your numbers are right? Sales seem kind of low."

"People don't buy much jewellery after Christmas." Alex rifled through more papers. "Here's photocopies of eight invoices received from Lions Imports in January and February of this year. That's practically an invoice a week, when Ice Craft normally buys stones from Lions maybe every three or four months at most." He placed the invoices before her. "Notice how Sam Roche consistently bought diamonds, rubies, emeralds, and sapphires between one and five carats in size."

"It's what I'd buy," Jillian said and slipped her fork under the scrambled eggs, "given the opportunity."

"His purchase orders don't look anything like Alfred Lin's normal transactions, though. I wonder if he had a reason for buying those particular stones."

"Eat your breakfast," Jillian said. "It looks wonderful. What's the red speckled stuff on the eggs?"

"Paprika."

She inhaled the sweet, smoky smell of golden brown sausages. "You like spicy food, don't you?"

"Love it." Alex retrieved his plate from the counter. "I heard Alfred Lin's difficult to deal with."

"He's reserved with people he doesn't know. He's a proud man, but once you get to know him he's grea—"

"Hold it! I thought I heard something."

"What? I didn't hear anything."

Alex put his plate down and tiptoed to the bedroom, returning moments later with the pistol.

"Expecting more rats?" She stared at the weapon.

"Just a bogeyman or two." He sat down, placed the gun on the chair next to him, then started to chop and mix his food. "How do your partners get along with one another?"

"There's been some personality clashes but nothing serious."

"What kind of personality clashes?"

"Well, Martin despised Craig McBride from the moment they met and tried to stop him from becoming a partner, but then he's tried to keep a lot of people from becoming partners at one point or another."

"Why?" He glanced at the door.

"He doesn't like to share responsibility. When John Morrow died, he thought he'd have more, but then Les made Isobel a partner."

Alex wiped a bit of egg from the corner of his mouth. "I heard that Craig hadn't been with the firm long before John helped him to the top."

Jillian looked at him. Somehow, she'd find out who was telling him this stuff.

"John and Craig got along really well. Les wasn't thrilled about John's decision, but there was no changing his mind."

Alex spread marmalade on his toast. "How does Martin deal with Craig now?"

"Not well. He thinks Craig's cheapened the profession." She shook her head and smiled. "Actually, he's jealous because Craig's popular with the C.A.s and about twenty years younger than he is. Martin's secretary says he's a misogynist, but I think he hates everybody."

"Have you clashed with him?"

"Not really." She watched Alex glance at the door again. "Course, he often acts as if I've done something wrong. Sometimes, when I'm looking through a file I'll spot him standing there glaring at me. It's creepy."

"Have you told Les about it?"

"He knows Martin spies on the staff," Jillian replied, as she sliced a sausage into tiny pieces, "but he doesn't take it seriously."

"Maybe Les doesn't know his partners well enough to see the truth about them. I asked him for a few basics the other day and he couldn't answer anything."

Jillian nodded. "Les makes 'won't' look like 'can't' better than anyone I know."

"He probably doesn't see them the same way you do."

"Why should he? The partners treat us differently. Around me they either relax or tense up, depending on the degree of brain damage they've suffered from being C.A.s too long." She picked up her toast. "You've got ketchup on your chin."

Alex dabbed his face with a serviette. "Would any of the partners have a reason for betraying Les?"

She looked at him. "Absolutely not. The firm's done well over the last few years: grown a lot."

She had reservations about the absolutely not part. Some things, certain conflicts, were undefinable, irreparable.

"Of course, Les has the last word on everything, but then he and John Morrow started the company; they took the initial risks."

"Do you think he wishes he could lose a couple of partners?"

"What I think about Les's actions is irrelevant."

"The perfect answer from a loyal employee." Alex removed his glasses and plunked them on the table. "But if you levelled with me we just might keep more people from dying."

Jillian swallowed a lump of toast. "What, exactly, do you mean?"

Staring at his plate, he felt as if someone had pinned his chest to the table. "Sam Roche was murdered last night."

Her knife and fork clattered onto her plate. "Oh, God."

"It was supposed to look like a drug overdose."

"What makes you think it wasn't?"

Les had told Alex about yesterday's meeting at Tony Barker's restaurant. He said Barker abruptly ended the meeting after Roche mentioned an island off the coast near Sechelt. Les hadn't yet discovered a reason for the island's significance, but he was sure one existed. Alex agreed. Tristan had loaned him Barker's personal tax file for twenty-four hours. In the file, scribbled notes referred to an unnamed island; notes that he'd begun to decipher with much more care.

After some hesitation, Les had also revealed that the numbers in the Lions financial statements he'd had printed out were significantly different from the final draft. He claimed not to have known who'd made the changes; on the other hand, he refused to hand the statements over because Jillian hadn't been returned to the office; a pretty lame excuse, Alex thought.

"Alex?"

He put his glasses back on. "Sam Roche hadn't made a lot of friends over the fraud, Jillian."

"A drug overdose sounds like something that would happen to him, though. A couple of times Sam came to our office buzzed out of his mind."

"Who did he come to see?"

"Les. He was always running errands for Alfred. Sometimes he'd pop in to have lunch with Craig."

Alex gazed absently at his plate. "They're friends?"

"Yeah, I guess. So, who'd want to kill Sam Roche?"

He scratched his chin. "Someone with a secret to protect. There's also the question of revenge."

Jillian hesitated. "Alfred Lin wouldn't kill anyone."

Alex returned her gaze. He wasn't so sure. Lin's desperate financial situation might have caused a confrontation with Roche. Since Roche's wrists hadn't been slashed, maybe there were two killers.

"Alex, where are you?" Jillian waved her hand in front

of him.

He took his plate to the sink. "Tell me what happened at work on Thursday, the day the phone calls started. You must have seen or heard something to do with the fraud."

Jillian stood up from the table. "Let me do the dishes. I feel like a couch potato." She didn't add that this was a normal state of affairs, since her walks rarely lasted more than twenty minutes.

"You've earned the right to a little pampering," he answered. "Considering what I've put you through, it's the least I can do."

"Alex, you'd be the perfect man if you didn't go around kidnapping women." She sat down. "When are you going to give all that manic energy a rest?"

"When this is all over."

"Maybe I'll make you a chocolate cheesecake. If you could get the ingredients, I'll pay for them."

Alex filled the sink with water, squirted in too much soap, and watched the suds rise. "Do you like to bake?"

"Yeah, but I'm not an expert by anyone's standards. Once, I made cream puffs and wound up poisoning my boyfriend's parents. I didn't know the cream was off."

Alex turned on the cold water tap, then quickly turned it off again. "Jillian, please tell me about last Thursday."

She watched him return to the files on the kitchen table. "It was a bad day. I had ten sets of financial statements to type, so I wasn't taking calls and hardly saw anyone until I went for dinner at seven."

"If you had a finalized set of statements in front of you, could you tell which partner had reviewed them?"

"Sure, by the handwriting on the auditor's report or the accountant's comments."

"If the statements weren't signed, could you still tell?"

"Probably. The partners disagree about statement wording and formatting, so rather than compromise each uses a slightly different style."

"Knowing the partners as well as you do, you'd be able to tell who'd written what."

Jillian gazed at the files on the table. She recognized the typed label on a folder she'd seen Jerry carry a hundred times. She picked up Tony Barker's personal tax file.

"Alex, this belongs to Jerry Margolin! He has nothing to do with the fraud, so what are you doing with it?"

"What makes you so sure of his innocence?"

Jillian plunked the file down. "Maybe if you stopped prying and putting everyone on the defensive, the Ice Craft mess might work itself out."

"What will work out for you, Jillian? Forty more years of clerical slavery before retirement? It's your life, my friend; you can stop renting it from Silby & Morrow anytime." He marched to the sink.

Hitching up her pyjama bottoms, Jillian followed him. "If Les trusts you so much then why doesn't he tell you who signed the statements?"

"Because there's been a screw-up and he's still trying to sort out the confusion."

"They were Craig's statements; his wording, everything."

Alex observed her. "Did you see Craig's signature?"

"No, but I knew they were his because I typed them."

"Did he give you the statements?"

"They just showed up on my desk, which is his usual routine."

"Jillian, is it remotely possible that someone else could have reviewed and changed the statements?"

"I suppose so." She strolled back to the files on the table. "How did you manage to get Barker's tax file?"

"It was easy." Alex rinsed a soapy plate.

"How easy?"

"Want a demonstration?"

"I'm not sure."

"Do you have a diary?"

Jillian rolled up her pyjama sleeves. "Why do you ask?"

"I'll show you." He walked to his bedroom and returned with Jillian's diary. "See how easy that was?"

"You are a conniving little creep!"

"If that's your attitude I want my pyjamas back."

She started to leave the room when Alex reached for her arm and held on.

"Listen to me." He adjusted his glasses. "Two people have been murdered because of a fraud investigation I was dumb enough to pursue alone. Now somebody wants us dead. You have the answers I need to get us out of trouble, so tell me, did anything unusual happen that Thursday evening?"

Jillian broke from his grasp, sat down again and opened the diary. The date of the last entry was over a month ago. She'd written four lines about the weather; afterward there'd been nothing else to say.

"Did you read it?"

"Jillian, *please* help me."

She wondered if she should she tell him she'd found Tony Barker standing in the reception area at eight o'clock that night. She didn't know how he'd gotten in when the elevators had been shut off two hours earlier.

Alex sat next to her. "Who, besides yourself, worked late Thursday night?"

"All the partners, plus several C.A.s and students. One of the more annoying ones, a guy named Tristan Wells, dropped by around quarter to eight to show his date where he worked. The jerk introduced me as his girl Friday."

Alex laughed. "I must have just missed that."

Jillian folded her arms. "If you were there, then why the hell are you asking me about Thursday night?"

"Les wanted me out of sight. I do know that Barker had a meeting with Jerry because Les was furious about the mess they left in the boardroom."

"Yeah, I know. He was still mad the next day."

She described the argument over the Scotch bottle, how

Les had held it in the air and yelled about the sticky paper stuck to the bottom of his most expensive bottle.

"Was anything written on the paper?"

She studied Alex closely. "You missed that one, did you? I wondered why half the crumpled sheets in the boardroom had been smoothed out by the time I started to clean up."

"You're catching on," he answered. "Very good."

"I'm beginning to understand how devious you are."

"What was on the paper?"

"A map of some sort. I couldn't figure out to where, though."

"Could you reproduce it?"

"Maybe," she replied, then paused. "Why?"

"I'll be back in a sec." He vanished for only a moment, then reappeared with a map of B.C.'s Sunshine Coast, acquired after Les mentioned the island. While Jillian drew the route, Alex tried to pinpoint the location of Barker's island near the Sechelt area.

"It must be one of those." He pointed to a group of dots.

"What?"

"Tony Barker's private island."

"What private island?"

"Les told me Barker owns an island."

"He did, did he? Then I suppose he'd already told you about the Scotch bottle. Thanks for all your trust, Alex."

"Jillian, I wasn't testing you. We went through everything in the boardroom that night but I didn't see any bottle. Les must have found it in the morning, then forgot to tell me about the map."

Alex suddenly rose from the table. Les had acted as if Roche's description was the first he'd heard about the island, yet Les must have already seen Barker's map stuck to the bottle. Surely he'd made the connection between the map and Roche's description.

Jerry Margolin obviously knew about the island. Had he mentioned it to Les in confidence earlier, or had he kept the information to himself?

As Alex finished washing the dishes, he told Jillian about Les's meeting at Barker's restaurant. He wanted to keep busy, away from her observation. She'd been watching him closely all weekend and might sense the doubts he'd begun to have about her boss. Les could have hidden the bottle from him that night. He'd been asked to wait while Les made sure Jerry and Barker had left the boardroom. Alex immersed his hands in the warm soapy water.

"I guess you do most of the memory work for Les," he said.

"Les is quite capable of remembering things, he just pretends otherwise."

"I thought he was an honest man." He could almost feel doubt pricking his knees and shoulders, scratching the back of his neck.

Jillian began opening drawers. "I'm not sure what he is lately, except miserable and remote."

"What are you doing?"

"Looking for a tea towel to dry your dishes."

"I told you; you don't have to do any work." Alex took her by the hand, and led her to the nearest chair. "Tell me about Les and how he is lately."

She frowned. "He makes me lie to clients. He tells them it's my fault if something goes out late or with mistakes. He expects me to work overtime for free and whenever he asks."

"You're angry, aren't you?" Alex returned to the sink.

"How I feel and what I think doesn't seem to count. All that matters these days is what Les thinks. The trouble is, when your whole life revolves around words like, 'the company recognizes its share of partnership income for the partnership's fiscal period ending with the company's fiscal period,' your outlook on life becomes a little warped. No one can understand you, and no one wants to, because they think it's all crap anyway, which it is, or so Les used to say," she attempted a smile and continued, "when he still had a sense of humour."

"Have you done something to upset him lately, like maybe seeing something you shouldn't have?" That would explain why Les wanted her back so badly.

Jillian folded Alex's map.

"Maybe he thinks you know too much," he suggested.

She took aim and threw the map at him. When it landed in the sink Alex swiftly patted the water off.

"You have a weird way of communicating, too, or is this the brain damage that comes from being a secretary too long?"

Hiking up her pyjama bottoms, Jillian marched into the living room. She opened the sliding glass door and stepped onto the balcony. A cool breeze swept over her.

Les could have upset his own staff, Alex thought. If Jillian was to catch anybody off guard, it would probably be Les. He was the one she was around the most. He also had easy access to her desk.

"Jillian?"

She gazed at three freighters anchored in the bluish grey water of English Bay. They were waiting to enter the inner harbour to pick up wheat or some other commodity. There were no sailboats out yet, but a couple of windsurfers in wet suits were already skimming along the light chop.

Alex joined Jillian on the balcony and made her face him.

"You're not very nice after all, are you?" she said.

"I'm a lot of things. Right now I'm concerned about you." He lightly stroked her arm. "Tell me more about Les."

"There's not much else to say." She gazed across the bay at the H.R. MacMillan Planetarium and wished she could roam through green, spacious Vanier Park that surrounded it. "I guess I'm supposed to figure out what's wrong with him, correct it, and apologize for both of us."

She turned to Alex. "Maybe you're what's wrong with him, plus the fraud and the murders; the danger they pose to his reputation." She thought of Jerry Margolin's relationship to Tony, the awkward position Jerry would be in if Tony was a criminal. "It doesn't sound like Les to let a stranger investigate his partners in the first place."

"He doesn't want the police to hear about the fraud until he knows what's going on." Or until he can cover his own ass, Alex thought.

Les had agreed, almost too readily, to his investigation, and why not? It was a convenient way of keeping his eye on things.

"Alex, who's working with you at Silby & Morrow?"

"Les knows what's going on."

"You knew exactly where to find me in the storage room. You also had someone take my purse out of my desk drawer and steal one of Jerry's files. Les wouldn't do that. Who is he, Alex?"

Alex removed his glasses and held them up to the light. "Why do you say 'he'?"

"Oh," she said, then gave him a broad smile. "Your spy's a woman."

He didn't answer her.

"And if Roche died last night then how did you get the news when I've been here with you all weekend?"

"I got a phone call after you passed out from the wine around midnight."

"I didn't pass out; I was exhausted."

"You had six glasses of wine and snored all through the late show. I could barely hear a word." He put his glasses back on. "I had to put you to bed."

"You could have woken me," she said. "Of course, your spy might have been hiding in the closet disguised as a large pair of running shoes. How long have you been friends?"

"Not long. It's been one of those whirlwind things, much like you and me."

"I doubt if anything's been like you and me." She looked at him. "I woke up at four this morning. While I was putting on these nifty pyjamas, I heard the TV. Were you watching something good, or did you fall asleep in front of it?"

"I had insomnia." Alex put his hands on Jillian's shoulders, then slipped them around her back. "Andy's funeral is this morning. I'll only be gone a couple of hours."

"Take your time," she answered gently, not daring to move. His embrace felt comforting. "Did you know him well?"

"We were best friends. Met in tenth grade. I helped him study. He helped me keep my feet on the ground."

"Would you like me to go with you?"

"I'd like you to help me search for clues to two murders. I thought we'd start on Tony Barker's island."

"Why?"

"To see what's so important about the place, and to talk to Barker. I heard he's there, and since you can't come up with the answers I need, then he'll have to."

Jillian's mouth dropped open. "Tony will recognize me!"

"Don't worry." Alex swept a strand of hair from her eyes. "I've got everything worked out, more or less."

"Will your friend be there, too?"

"No."

He hurried back to the kitchen, and let the water out of the sink. He wanted to keep Tristan out of danger because he couldn't cope with one more loss. Auditors weren't trained to deal with tragedy and nothing could really prepare them for it. Blood was for cops and surgeons, violence for prison guards; people who weren't emotionally paralyzed by death. Alex's world was supposed to contain sane, ambitious types whose worst crime was to cook books and vote for socialism.

As Jillian strolled into the kitchen, he said, "Maybe you should start packing, and take the green dress in the closet because I hear Tony's lodge is no ordinary cabin."

"I figured it wouldn't be if you're interested in it." She fumbled with her pyjama bottoms. "Sometimes you're really strange, Alex."

"I have a murder suspect in mind. A man with a good reason for wanting Sam Roche dead."

"Who?"

Considering the scrutiny Andy had given the Lions Imports financial records, Barker must have thought Andy suspected him. Andy had described Barker as a big man, someone too large to have been the assailant behind the face mask. Maybe he got nervous and had Andy killed, then sent the killer to finish Alex off.

It explained the existence of the man in a black raincoat: a stranger who appeared unexpectedly in parking lots, office stairwells, and alleys. It could also explain Sam Roche's death, since he was a man who probably knew a lot more about Barker than he'd told. Compounding the problem, however, were the different ways Andy and Sam Roche had died. Were there really two killers?

Alex removed his glasses and rubbed his eyes.

"Who's your suspect, Alex?"

He put his glasses back on and looked at Jillian's raised eyebrows. Compassion softened her expression. Beneath the scowls and contemptuous gazes, she really was beautiful. If he had more time, if finding a killer wasn't so vital. . . . He wasn't sorry about pulling Jillian into this, because in some strange way, her presence was therapeutic.

"I can't give you a name yet, not without proof."

It was the kind of thing Andy would have said, only his funeral was today. Monty and Ida Gowan would be burying their son.

"Do you think the killer will be on the island?"

"It's possible."

"We're doomed."

"Don't worry, you'll be perfectly safe."

Alex couldn't blame her for her scepticism, that revealed itself in those folded arms and light green eyes, narrowed like a cat who found the sunlight just a touch too bright.

TWENTY

Kelly Faust enjoyed breaking rules. It made him feel powerful, wise, and unbeatable. Social protocol had always been his favourite target. Long after he'd taken accounting courses to climb out of the mail room, he still preferred the company of mail clerks to auditors. Over recent months, he'd broken much more serious rules: something that was not only necessary, but justified.

After his father died, Kelly spoke with the people who'd known Victor Faust. He'd wanted to understand how a man as vicious as his father had been able to wander among normal, respectable people for nearly four decades without being recognized for what he was. He'd learned that colleagues had been fooled by his father's passive facade, and that no one wanted to hear about his darker side. It had become Kelly's mission to teach these people about the darker side of human beings, without resorting to physical violence. It was much more fitting to implicate them in scandals.

He started by blackmailing the occasional taxpayer he caught cheating on his or her taxes. It hadn't taken long to realize that business people who cheated the government tended to cheat other people in all sorts of ways. He was happy to allow these individuals to continue their scams, for a price. By forging signatures to carefully worded documents, he'd created what appeared to be a ring of extortionists and blackmailers run by a small number of top-level people. His father's colleagues, those who'd passed him by for promotions, would soon be forced to explain their way out of large, private bank accounts plus documented evidence of blackmail and extortion efforts.

If the truth did surface at some point, Kelly would be far removed from the picture by then, living anonymously on a portion of the profits gathered from crooks. His pending lay-off would save him from having to explain what could be perceived as a timely resignation. All the documents were now ready and waiting for him to hand over to the media once Alex Bellamy stopped prying into the Ice Craft affair. No one, except perhaps Alex and Jillian Scott, could stop Kelly from doing as he pleased anymore, which was why he sat here in a Silby & Morrow office, peering across the desk at a shaken and worried partner.

"Do you have my glasses?" Kelly asked.

His contact avoided his gaze. "They're not here, and you shouldn't be either. It's too risky."

He smiled. "I want you to come to Tony Barker's island with me."

"Impossible."

Kelly adjusted his father's round, wire-framed glasses. They were too large for him, but at least he could see. A vision problem was all they'd had in common.

"I want to find out what he's doing over there firsthand, and to make sure he hasn't told anyone about you."

"You didn't tell Tony I'd visit the island, did you?"

"I sent him a private and confidential letter on your behalf, saying you and I must see him urgently."

His contact stared at him.

"You'll be kept out of sight until the right moment, I assure you."

"I can't do it."

"Yes, you can. I'll even supply a disguise to protect you, just in case other familiar faces are there."

"It won't work, Kelly. I've decided to tell the partners

the truth and take my chances with them."

He leaned across the desk and grabbed his contact's arm. "Your partners won't back you. They want your career ruined. I have a letter from one of them telling me you falsified the Lions Imports tax returns and financial statements."

His contact stared at him. "That had better be a bad joke."

"The letter was signed with just the firm's name, but it didn't take long to discover who your enemy was and probably still is."

"Which is how, with five partners to choose from," his contact remarked bitterly, "you picked me to make sure Sam Roche's fraud wasn't detected too quickly."

"Unfortunately," he answered, "you blew it."

"Who wrote the letter, Kelly?"

"I compared the signature with those on your colleagues' personal income tax returns. I also compared it with your forged signature on the Lions statements. Anyone with a little intelligence would know you signed them, and whose signature you tried to make it look like," Kelly remarked. "You should have spent more time practicing forging signatures. It takes time to get it right."

His contact glared at him.

"I imagine the letter writer has been wondering why you and Barker weren't investigated before now." Kelly released his grip, then slowly leaned back in his chair and sighed. "You can't walk away from me, you know. It's not in the rules, and if you break my rules I'll pull you right out of the game, understand?"

He watched fear and alarm merge into a whole and perfect terror on his contact's face.

"I'll pick you up at your place at six this evening. Be ready to go by then." Faust stood up. "One more thing. Where's your copy of the Lions financial statements?"

His contact hesitated.

"You were to bring them here, remember?"

"They're around somewhere. Things have been chaotic because of Jillian's absence."

"Have a quick look." Kelly sat down again. "I'll wait."

A couple of drawers were searched, the desk top scarcely looked at before the flustered partner met his eyes. "Actually, they're gone."

"Since when?"

"I was in the coffee room early this morning, looking them over while waiting for the coffee to brew. A C.A. came up to me and asked for a file from my office. I left the statements on top of the refrigerator and went with the kid."

"Why did you leave them there?"

"Obviously, I didn't want him to know I had them. When I returned three minutes later, the statements were gone."

"Nobody mentioned finding the material?"

"No."

"You'd better identify Alex Bellamy's accomplice fast, hadn't you? If he gives them to Alex, your career's over." Kelly stood up. "You *will* go to the island. I've waited twenty-five years to put my life in order. Nobody's going to upset things now."

His contact sat down, too panic-stricken to respond.

TWENTY-ONE

Jerry sat in his office, thinking about what had happened yesterday when Marlena threw her clothes in a suitcase and left for Tony's island. It was too much; too much was going wrong, first with the Ice Craft trouble, then Jillian's disappearance, and now Sam Roche's death. Marlena had insisted he accompany her and Tony to the island. When he refused, she had stormed out of the house. Now, Les wanted to know why he hadn't joined his wife, and Jerry couldn't remember having told him she'd left. He must have done so last night, when Les called to tell him about Roche's death.

"Will you be talking to Marlena soon?" Les asked.

But Marlena was here, whispering in his ear, needing him, she said.

"Jerry, have you been to Tony's island?"

Les was annoyed with his partner's distracted silence. Before he met Marlena, Jerry had been alert and independent, yet at the wedding he'd behaved like a naïve adolescent pledging to leap off a cliff with his bride. He hadn't seen the bride step back, hadn't heard the tone of insincerity in her marriage vows. He still wasn't thinking clearly.

"No, Les," he answered softly, "I've never been there."

"When you do go, I'd like to come along."

Jerry stared at him. "Why?"

"Barker's secrecy about the island is a problem for both of us, I think. The sooner we clear it up the sooner things can return to normal."

"Is the island a problem, Les, or just Tony?"

"What am I supposed to think about a man like Barker? Why did he end Saturday's meeting when Roche mentioned the island? What is so damn important about that place?"

"I don't know."

Les watched him closely. "If you knew this office had released a falsified set of financial statements to Tony Barker, would you have corrected the situation, even if it meant offending Barker?"

Jerry flicked the beads on the jade abacus he used as a paperweight. "What do you think?"

"If I knew, I wouldn't have asked."

Les left the room, convinced it had been necessary to shake Jerry up. He'd become uncommunicative at a time when Les most needed his cooperation. He wished he'd made Roche name the partner involved in the fraud; however, just before Saturday's meeting he'd reviewed the Lions statements and was so upset by the numbers that his attention had become more focused on Barker than Roche. Now Roche was dead, Barker had retreated to his island, and all he could do was run around trying to bully the truth out of people.

Les opened Isobel's door and found her writing on one of the dozen notepads scattered over her desk. She held a cigarette in her left hand, and had a full cup of coffee in front of her. Isobel looked up, bleary-eyed, her courtesy chipped and peeling. Since she usually hated Monday mornings, Les decided it would be wiser to approach the Lions subject later, when her mood would be brighter.

"Isobel, are you free for lunch?"

"Tomorrow."

"Fine." He left quickly and, hearing laughter from Craig's office, barged inside. The man with Craig was one of his classier clients: the owner of a used car lot.

Craig's smile drooped into a joyless, bored expression, as if unannounced intrusions were a common occurrence.

Les couldn't forgive his partner for the life he led in sleazy hotels, couldn't respect a man who'd cheated on his wife.

"Mr. McBride."

"Mr. Silby, and how's Jillian? Back at work yet?"

"No. Have you and Martin sorted out the T1 situation?"

"I tried first thing this morning, but he'd shut himself in his office and wouldn't let me in. I think he's finally losing his mind." Craig winked at the client, who smiled and turned his back on Les.

Les stared at his partner. He didn't appreciate Craig's flippancy.

"Did you hear about Sam Roche?" Les knew they were drinking buddies. Lately, he'd begun to wonder just how friendly they'd been.

"No," Craig answered with mild interest. When he saw Les look at the client, he added, "Go ahead. You can talk in front of Bill. He's very discreet."

Les sighed. "Sam died of a drug overdose on Saturday night. Apparently, the police couldn't locate his family, so when they learned that he'd worked for Ice Craft, they called Alfred to get hold of Sam's personnel file. Alfred called me yesterday."

"I guess Alfred will be happy," Craig remarked, "not to mention a few other people."

As Les closed the door he noticed that Craig looked rather upset by the news.

When he entered Martin's office without knocking, Les was startled by his appearance. Grey creases hung in folds below his cheekbones. Blue bags bulged under his eyes and a red vertical line had appeared between his brows.

"You look ill, Martin."

"I am," he said, staring at Les, "and what do you think is killing me?"

Les didn't answer.

"The police have no record of any kidnapping," he continued, "and you were just a little too calm about it, Leslie."

"What are you implying?"

"That you know more about this situation than you've told us."

"I know that she was taken against her will. You saw that yourself, Martin. And I know that she's safe where she is now." Les stared at him. "What did you tell the police?"

"Nothing, and I looked bloody foolish because of it." He wiped his face with a handkerchief. "I have to go for tests this afternoon, for my heart. I'll be in tomorrow."

"If you need more time off, take it."

"I couldn't, not with my wife hovering about," he said, and sighed loudly. "I remember our vacations. She'd be decent the first day, grumpy the next. By the end of the week she'd be hitting me in public, for God's sake."

Les doubted that Martin had done much for her vacations either. "Can I get you anything? A glass of water? Tea?"

"Thank you, no. Now, if you'll excuse me, I have work to finish before my appointment."

"Actually, I came to find out if you'd heard about Sam Roche." He'd also intended to tell him about the falsified numbers on the Lions Imports financial statements. Now he wasn't sure Martin could cope with much more bad news.

"Jerry told me about Mr. Roche first thing this morning," he answered irritably. "I'm sorry for the man, but it's just one more nasty twist in the whole sordid business. Maybe we can finally put all of this behind us." He opened a file. "I really must get this work done."

In his own office, Les removed a staff phone list from his desk drawer and studied each of the names, checking off the five people he distrusted most. Tristan Wells was the only non-partner among them.

He decided to go to Barker's island and sort things out with the man once and for all. If he'd done so earlier then maybe he wouldn't feel so damn responsible for every disaster that had touched his firm lately, and maybe he wouldn't feel so terrified about what could happen next.

TWENTY-TWO

The forest on either side of the highway rushed past Jillian, and the wind rubbed the side of her face raw. She pressed a button, making the car window slide shut. Alex pressed a button and the window slid down again. She closed it. Alex opened it. They battled like this until the window shuddered to a stop and stayed there, half open.

"What do you think you're doing?" she asked.

"Trying to keep you alert."

"You broke the window."

"There's a blanket on the back seat if you're cold."

Jillian pulled the blanket around her, then peered into the darkness along this winding, two-lane highway.

"How much farther is it to Sechelt?"

"About five minutes."

Jillian looked at her watch. The ferry ride from Horseshoe Bay to Langdale had taken forty-five minutes. They'd been driving for nearly half an hour and during all that time Alex had barely spoken.

He'd been more paranoid than usual since his friend's funeral. A couple of times last night he'd turned the lights off in the apartment and gazed out the window at the street below. Whenever Jillian had asked what was wrong he'd either replied, "nothing," or shut himself in his bedroom and made phone calls.

On the ferry, she'd asked if something had gone wrong

at the funeral. Alex's response was to take her arm, and march her around the deck while he stared at people. Now back in the car, the rear-view mirror held his attention.

"Is someone following us?" She turned around.

"Not yet."

"Why are you so edgy then?"

"I have a lot on my mind."

At the cemetery, Andy's mom, Ida, had put her arm around him, and told him the cuts to Andy's wrists were apparently too neat and too deep to have been self-inflicted. It also seemed that Andy had been struck on the head and jaw with a blunt object. After pleading unsuccessfully for an explanation, Ida informed Alex he could expect a police visit soon. She'd also learned that Revenue Canada was about to report his disappearance and the absence of a couple of audit files. Breaking from Ida's grasp, Alex had run away.

"Tell me what's on your mind, Alex. Maybe I can help."

"It'd help if you talked about the partners."

She didn't know where to begin, what to say. She gazed out her window at the lights of sporadically placed houses at the edge of the forest. On the other side of the street the ocean was suddenly closer. She looked at him.

"You never told me if you have any brothers or sisters."

"Two brothers and two sisters."

"Do they live in Vancouver?"

"In other parts of the world. Have you ever been anything besides a secretary?"

"I was a human being, once."

"It's that bad, is it?"

She shrugged. "It used to be fun, when the staff liked one another. Now everyone's operating on personal agendas at the expense of other people's careers and self-esteem."

"Why don't you quit?"

"It recently dawned on me that I don't want to be a secretary anymore, but I don't know what I want to do."

"I know the feeling."

She looked at him. "That first night in the tunnel, you told me you used to work at the Carnegie Centre. What'd you do there?"

"I was the janitor. I've also picked berries during the summer and worked at McDonalds, where I was an especially good bun man."

"I'm sure you were."

He relaxed his grip on the steering wheel. "I've driven an ice cream truck and baby-sat too. In my early teens, I worked at a resort on one of the Gulf Islands."

"How did you get a job like that?"

"My parents owned the resort. We lived on Salt Spring Island until I was fifteen, when they sold the place to buy a hotel in Vancouver. Two years later they sold that hotel to buy a bigger one in Montreal."

His parents had wanted him to go with them. With one year left before high school graduation, he'd insisted on staying in British Columbia. He also wanted to stay near his grandmother because she'd grown frightened of ending her days alone in a hospital.

His parents claimed they hadn't realized how ill she was until after the contracts had been signed and all their property sold. It was true that she'd never looked ill, but Alex had seen the slowing of her movements, small grimaces when she stood up. He'd listened as her nostalgic stories slowly became incoherent ramblings. He used to wonder why they hadn't seen the signs until, at her funeral, he realized they probably had and just couldn't face the truth. None of them had taken her death particularly well, but his dad had been the hardest hit: guilt-ridden for not being there.

"What was the resort on Salt Spring like?"

"Far more rustic than Barker's mansion. He runs his place like an exclusive club. Guests are given one of these cards," Alex said, showing her what looked like a credit card, "to get inside."

"Where did you get the card?"

"It was in Barker's personal tax file, along with scribbled notes that didn't make sense until Les mentioned the island. Anyway, I arranged an invitation for you and me."

"How?"

"Through a friend. Confirmation of our acceptance came last night, along with more information about the place."

Tristan had also given him the missing Lions Imports financial statements, which he'd found on top of the refrigerator in Silby & Morrow's coffee room. Unfortunately, he hadn't seen who'd left them there. After studying the statements, Alex knew Special Investigations had enough evidence for either prosecution or blackmail. He couldn't wait to hear what Mr. Barker had to say about it.

"When did you get the information? No one came to the apartment last night."

"My friend met me in the lobby. Remember when I told you I had to take the garbage out?"

"Oh, Mr. Bond, how clever you are! I thought the garbage was real! It smelled real."

"Jillian, this isn't a game. We're looking for white-collar criminals involved in two murders."

"I've been giving that some thought, actually, and I doubt if your fraud suspects killed anybody."

Alex sighed. "Think about motives, circumstances, timing, and relationships."

"I've read that criminals don't usually mix their crimes, though. Car thieves don't rob banks, for instance; bank robbers don't become arsonists; and white-collar criminals don't slit peoples' wrists. Everyone specializes."

As they entered Sechelt, Jillian looked at the vacated streets and partially illuminated buildings. Salt air swept in through her half-open window. Between buildings, she caught a glimpse of a moonlit beach.

"Have any of the partners run into fraud cases before?" he asked.

"Not that I know of. Is that relevant?"

"I don't think you understand how serious commercial crime is. Left unchecked, nobody's bank account, credit card, or credit rating will be safe."

"If I went back to work maybe I could learn something there."

Alex glanced at the rear-view mirror. A vehicle was approaching at top speed. Its high beams pierced the car with light.

"You're afraid to go to Barker's island, aren't you?"

"Damn right!" Jillian looked out the window and squinted in the wind. "If I get shot because of you, I trust you'll go on to save the economy without me."

The headlights were ten feet away. Alex steadily applied the brakes until he was well below the speed limit. He looked at the passing car. The woman's head scarcely rose above the steering wheel.

"Why don't you let the fraud cops handle this?" she added. "Judging from the numbers and invoices you showed me at the apartment, they've got a good reason to investigate. The deaths of two people would involve the homicide guys, too."

Alex was reluctant to point out that he was probably high on the cops' suspect list in Andy's death. The wounds on his face would make investigators wonder if they'd fought, if he'd exploded in some sort of rage.

"I need more evidence to link the fraud with the murders before they'll take me seriously. That's why I haven't called them."

"Isn't it their job to find the evidence?"

"I doubt if the cops have the time and manpower to find it."

"How do you know?"

"I learned some things about the force when I once thought about joining it."

Jillian looked at him. "Why didn't you?"

"I was told that candidates had to know how to swim."

"You couldn't take lessons?"

"Didn't want to."

"How come?"

Alex tapped the steering wheel. "When I was seven, I was dumped upside down in a canoe and haven't been in the water since."

"Yet you'll cross it to nail a Silby & Morrow partner."

"To nail Andy's killer."

"Why did you want to become a cop?"

"For the excitement, I guess, and a sense that I'd be doing something useful. Besides, you don't get anywhere in life without taking risks. Course, when the risks can kill you a thousand different ways, you have to think twice."

"Have you been thinking twice about risks lately?"

He sighed and shook his head. "I didn't know things would go this far. Anyway, it's too late to turn back. The killer won't stop coming after us unless we make him stop."

Jillian shivered under the blanket. "I'd just be careful before I went around accusing Tony Barker of anything."

Alex glanced at her. "You think Barker's involved too, don't you?"

"All I know is that it takes a lot of money to own an island."

Alex also knew Barker had someone protecting his interests. The presence of the stranger in the black raincoat still bothered him. Had the guy planned to meet someone when the altercation in the stairwell occurred, or had Barker ordered him to steal the Lions file? Alex recalled the rumours about improper behaviour in Special Investigations, a troublemaker in the division; someone who might have had the means and the guts to blackmail Sam Roche and Barker for a cut of the fraud's profit. Someone capable of murder?

"Alex, you've drifted away again."

"Sorry." He glanced at the houses that had replaced the shops and offices. "Has Les Silby talked to anyone from Revenue Canada in the last few weeks?"

"Only one, as far as I know," she replied, as she tucked the blanket under her legs, "and he's afraid of rats and water."

Alex pulled onto the shoulder of the road, stopped the car and gazed at the rear-view mirror. Jillian turned around but nothing was there. She watched him take a sheet of paper from his pocket and study it carefully.

"Don't tell me we're lost."

"I'm just going over the last part of our route."

"Need some help?"

He kept his eyes on the paper. "I need you to tell me about your partners' personalities, likes and dislikes, emotional conflicts: that sort of thing."

"I wish I could give you detailed profiles. The truth is, they don't talk to me that much."

"I'll settle for astute impressions."

Jillian thought about this a moment. "I'll try."

Alex smiled. "So, who do you think is the toughest partner emotionally?"

"Les."

"And the weakest?"

"Martin Sloane has the worst time staying on his feet. He takes all of his problems to Les." She turned to him. "Still, knowing when to ask for help shows some strength of character."

Alex started driving again. "Who doesn't like asking for help?"

"Craig, but with him it's laziness. He believes in the least amount of work for the largest amount of billings."

"Does he over-bill?"

"You mean is he worth the two hundred bucks an hour he charges people? I doubt it."

"What about Jerry?"

"Worth every penny he earns."

"Does he have any weaknesses or quirks?"

"None."

Alex glanced at her. "Do you think he'd ever go against Les's wishes?"

"No."

Jillian wasn't sure if this was true, but she didn't want the question to lead to Jerry and Barker's friendship. Alex might start wondering how close they were and whether Jerry had done certain favours for Barker.

He slowed down a little to examine the driveways and open spaces leading from the road.

"If we caught the murderer," she said, "then you wouldn't have to waste time chasing a partner who'll have to answer to the Institute of Chartered Accountants anyway, right?"

"There you go again. Protecting the partners."

"I owe them loyalty, Alex. I've had promotions and earn a pretty good salary. If a rough patch comes along, it doesn't mean I spill my guts."

"Spill your guts?" Alex grinned.

"Never mind." She pulled the blanket around her shoulders.

"Tell me about Isobel Cameron's weaknesses. How does she handle herself around the office?"

"Maturely and responsibly."

"Surely in a profession where maybe five percent of the women make it to senior positions and even less to partnerships, she has added pressure, unless she's working with some progressive-thinking guys."

"They're not progressive. Martin treats her like a secretary, Craig sexually harasses her, and Jerry just tries to stay out of her way. Les is the only one who isn't threatened by her, but then he respects women who play it straight. I always thought they'd make a nice couple."

"Are they close?"

"Les can't cope with emotional involvement, which is his greatest weakness. Still, I wouldn't want to cross him. All of the partners have strengths to counter their weaknesses, and when they want something they usually get it."

Alex lightly tapped the steering wheel in time to a tune on the radio. "What if they all want what only one can have?"

"Les steps in."

Alex scanned the ocean-side properties. Some of the lots were fairly large in this area; the driveways were far apart and poorly marked.

"Would any of the partners ever leave Silby & Morrow?"

Jillian didn't want to discuss partners anymore. The topic made her uncomfortable, and she wasn't sure what Alex would do with the information.

"All most public C.A.s want is to run their own firms."

"A lot of worries go with the job, though. The danger of releasing incorrect financial statements, or being forced to do something slightly unethical for an influential client with big bucks to pay."

"Les wouldn't put himself in that position." She tucked the blanket around her shoulders once more. "None of them would."

"What if Jerry had a chance to exchange partnership responsibilities for a less stressful, better-paying job in industry?"

Tristan had told him about the latest rumour to circulate around Silby & Morrow.

"Jerry likes and respects Les. He'd never leave."

Alex suddenly stopped the car and threw it into reverse. He backed up several yards, and turned into what appeared to be a trail between driveways.

"What are you doing?" Jillian asked. "The sign says "private: no thru road."

"I know. This is Tony Barker's special access to the beach. Tell me about Jerry's wife."

She looked at him. "Why?"

"She could be on the island."

"Oh no!" The blanket slipped from her shoulder.

"I don't want her to see you."

"Fine. I'll stay in the car while you row over."

He drove slowly over dirt and gravel, and dipped into the occasional pothole. Branches scraped the car. Leaves swished past the open window. Jillian leaned closer to Alex to avoid getting poked.

"What's wrong with Mrs. Margolin?" he asked.

"Nothing."

"Okay, Jillian, let's hear it. Don't hold back on me now."

"There's nothing to say, except her whole life revolves around looking good and being shallow."

"That sounds objective."

"It's a fact; ask anyone in the office. Marlena's one of those females who lives for men and wants nothing to do with women, unless she can use them to get at the men, or if she's been left stranded somewhere, which has probably never happened. I doubt if she could handle living alone."

"How do you handle it?"

"Just fine, thanks."

"You've never considered marriage?"

"I was proposed to twice."

"Impressive."

"By the same man."

"Oh?"

"After I poisoned his parents with the cream puffs, my boyfriend proposed over the phone two days later. A week after that, his parents told me Carl wasn't ready for marriage. Carl was furious and proposed to me again in front of them; that time I said no. His parents were right, he wasn't ready and my life would have been miserable trying to prove them wrong."

"What do you do with your time between marriage proposals?"

"I swim like a porpoise," she answered, then smiled.

"Good, you can jump into the boat after untying it."

He pulled the car to a stop. Fifty feet ahead was the ocean.

TWENTY-THREE

As Jillian stepped onto the pier, Alex fumbled around in the motor boat.

"Alex, what are you doing?"

"Trying to hide my gun. Weapons aren't allowed on the island."

"Why is it even an issue? What kind of people come here?" She looked beyond the pier, at what appeared to be nothing but forest.

"Would you take our suitcase, please?" he asked, then handed it to her.

Glancing at the water, Alex stumbled out of the boat. The pier was quiet, the island higher and larger than he'd expected.

They walked past a number of boats and up a dozen wooden steps. From there, a dirt path bordered by bushes and trees led them to a locked, eight-foot-high iron gate. A small light was attached to one side of the gate, but otherwise the area was lifeless and quiet.

"A wispy night in the enchanted forest." Jillian shoved her hands into her pockets. "Charming."

Alex walked up to the light and inserted the plastic card in the slot below it. Immediately the gates slid open. They walked up another set of wooden steps that brought them before a large three-storey structure. Lights could be seen behind the second-floor curtains, and porch lights illuminated the entrance.

"Can you believe this?" Jillian stared at the windows.

He glanced behind him. "Let's look around."

Alex walked behind Jillian, watching and listening for voices. Although he couldn't see anyone, he felt crowded and uneasy. He guided Jillian to the left and would have walked around the building but another set of gates, unequipped for plastic cards, kept him from continuing. Through the bars, more light shone between the cracks of second and third-floor curtains. There was no sign of movement; no one seemed to belong to the boats at the pier. They returned to the front of the building.

"I don't want to go in there," Jillian said.

"Don't worry, you'll be perfectly safe. Trust me."

"Alex." She clung to his arm and tried to pull him away, but he didn't budge.

"We're going inside, and please just go along with whatever I say, okay?"

"What trouble are you about to get us into now?"

"I'm not sure. Kind of makes things exciting, don't you think?"

"I feel nauseous."

Alex inserted the card in the front door, then ushered Jillian into a small panelled foyer cluttered with beaten-up furniture and mounted animal heads. The man entering through the door on their left looked out of place in his dark blue suit. He was tall and balding, his face partially hidden behind a thick grey moustache.

"Good evening. My name is John Forbes."

"Hello." The cuts on Alex's face puckered slightly as he smiled. "We're Mr. and Mrs. Reeves."

Jillian's eyes widened as she turned to Alex. He could have warned her.

"Welcome to the Lodge," Forbes said. "Your suite's in the east wing, this way."

Using a card identical to Alex's, he unlocked a second

162   Taxed to Death

door and entered a long hallway furnished with marble floors and dark oil portraits. Another man, similar in age and height to Forbes, stood at the foot of a wide, plushly carpeted staircase. He took the suitcase from Alex and bounded upstairs ahead of them.

On the second floor, they were led through the north, then the east wing until Forbes stopped midway down the corridor. At the end of the east wing, two people stood before another set of doors. They were formally dressed and stepping into a room filled with noise that was silenced as the doors closed behind them. After opening their suite, Forbes handed Alex the room key plus a second card.

"Enjoy your honeymoon, and all the best."

Jillian smiled as Forbes and his assistant left them alone.

"Honeymoon?" She raised her eyebrows.

"We won't be disturbed that way."

He strolled to the centre of a massive square room decorated in blue, green and yellow pastels. A white marble fireplace filled the wall on their right. Alex slowly turned around while Jillian wandered to the bar that ran the length of the wall opposite the fireplace.

"Would you like a drink, bridegroom?" She walked behind the bar. "I could use a Scotch."

"Orange juice will be fine."

"That's it?"

"Got to stay healthy and alert tonight." He turned his back to her.

"What happens if Tony Barker drops by to congratulate us?"

"We're a honeymooning couple who've just arrived from Europe and it's long past our bedtime." He gazed at a small ebony table. "By the time he shows up, we'll probably be back in Vancouver."

"Wonderful. My first honeymoon," she said, pouring the orange juice, "and it's worth about half a sentence in the diary."

Alex peeked out the window then drew the curtain back completely. Taking the juice from Jillian, he studied a landscaped courtyard brightened by tiny white lights. A dining room occupied the third floor of the wing across the courtyard. The couple they'd seen step into the noisy room would have entered the south wing, yet every floor was in darkness.

"Mr. Barker spares no expense for his friends," Jillian remarked, "or do they pay for all this?"

"Indirectly."

She looked at him. "Does Tony know any Mr. or Mrs. Reeves?"

"No. His wife sent him a telegram from France introducing us."

"How did you manage that?"

"One of my brothers lives in England: London, actually. He arranged everything after my friend found out that Barker's wife has been on an extended vacation in Paris."

"Did your friend arrange the boat for us?"

"Yes."

"She sounds like quite the organizer."

"He."

"I thought your friend was a woman."

"I know." He gulped the juice down and plunked the glass on the nearest table. "Did it bother you?"

"Did you want it to?"

He shrugged. "I'm not sure."

Jillian left the window and wandered around the room until she noticed a display case containing a collection of silver spoons and salt cellars. She bent down to examine the bottom of the pieces through the glass shelf.

"Alex, look at this." She pointed to the salt cellars. "They're authentic antiques."

While Alex peered at the case, he casually put his arm around her. "How can you tell?"

"By the design and marking on the bottom of the pieces."

She felt his hand lightly stroke her arm and didn't dare move, afraid that even a deep breath would stop him.

"The salt cellars are from the early nineteenth century. The tiny anchor engraved on that one," she pointed to a salt cellar sitting on four oval feet, "is the hallmark of the Birmingham Assay Office." Gently, she moved a little closer to him. "The lion beside it was used to verify the silver is sterling, and the sovereign's head showed that duty was paid on the piece. There's a date on it, a letter of the alphabet, but I'd have to look it up to identify the year."

"So, do you learn about this stuff between marriage proposals?" Alex drifted away from her. "It would explain all the antiques in your apartment."

"The silver jester holding the bells is a baby's rattle," she stated, then smiled. "His ivory legs were used for teething; very soothing for baby's frayed nerves."

As Jillian pushed up her sleeves, a tissue popped out. "If Tony can afford antiques for guest rooms he must be worth a fortune."

"Your tissue's on the floor again." Alex scanned the room. "I wonder how much Les knows about this place."

She sat down on the sofa. "I feel like I've intruded on something personal here."

"You have, but if it's to help the partners then the cause is worth it, right?"

"Sure."

Alex studied the paintings on each side of the fireplace. In the painting on the right the roses were pale yellow; on the left they were light pink.

"Jillian, if you had to choose a guilty partner, who would it be?"

"That's not a fair question."

Alex looked at her cardigan. "You shouldn't keep your hand in your pockets. It'll stretch the material."

Absently, she lifted her hand out.

"Is Martin Sloane capable of murder?" he asked.

"He's too much of a coward. Besides, it'd tarnish that respectable image he loves to shine in everyone's face."

"What about Isobel Cameron and Craig McBride?"

Jillian stared into her Scotch glass. "I don't know."

He played with the light switches, dimming them, then turning them up bright. "Is Les Silby a murderer?"

"No way. He prides his professional and moral standards as much as Martin does." Her hand slipped back in her pocket.

"What better way to remove suspicion than to hide behind a self-righteous image, and why is your hand in your pocket again?"

"It's just a reflex action; don't worry about it." She sipped her Scotch. "My father used to smack them with his belt when he thought they weren't busy enough with housework."

Alex noted her nonchalant expression, then wandered into the bedroom.

"Jillian, there's champagne in here, and the bed's been turned down."

The bedroom was cozy and elegant. As he stepped into the adjoining bathroom, Jillian strolled to the window on the far side of the room, and sat on the bed. She placed her glass on the night table, next to a vase filled with orange rosebuds.

As she gazed at the peach-coloured walls and pale green drapes, she tried to remember the faces and events of the past month; every awkward and strange situation that could establish a connection between honest people and a murderer. If a partner was involved then he wasn't involved willingly; she was certain of that, absolutely positive, no doubt in her mind at all, and at the very worst, nothing could be proved. So Jerry had some connection to Barker? So what? And she didn't think Les would have become involved with Sam Roche regardless of any blackmail threat. He'd despised Roche. Jillian rocked back and forth slightly as she stared at the orange rosebuds. Had Les despised Roche enough to want him dead?

"Alex?" She didn't want to think about Les anymore. "You never told me if you have a girlfriend." She ran her hand over the bed's white satin quilt.

"Romance isn't my strong suit. God knows I've tried."

"Keep trying," she murmured.

"What?"

"Nothing."

"Could you put the green dress on, please?"

Jillian opened the suitcase and removed a carefully folded garment. Dark green silk slipped through her hands. The dress was gorgeous, but she'd never have purchased something this sensuous. No guts for it, or had Alex assumed this and bought the dress to embarrass her?

When her blue jeans were off, Jillian took a large sip of Scotch, then removed her cardigan and blouse. Alex emerged from the bathroom wrapped in a small towel and Jillian covered herself with the dress. After four days of living with a modest, fairly reserved guy, she was shocked by his appearance. Of course, they'd never had to share a bedroom before.

"Do you want to use the shower?" He put his glasses on, then gazed at the dress.

"I don't know. Is any hot water left?"

"I took a cold shower." He rubbed his hair with a hand towel. "One of many, lately."

Jillian tried to suppress a smile. "Oh?"

"Can't let certain distractions get in the way."

The gold cross dangling down his chest flickered as he strolled to the suitcase. His legs and chest were more muscular than she'd imagined. Grabbing her make-up bag off the bed, Jillian hurried towards the bathroom.

"My God! What a becoming outfit!"

Alex grinned at the green and yellow striped knee socks she could shoot herself for not removing. She'd spent her whole life removing the wrong clothes first. The habit had become her largest humiliation when a lover would lunge at her semi-clad body before she'd removed the last sock.

"Given the size of that towel," Jillian raised an eyebrow, "are you sure you feel qualified to judge me?"

He laughed as he turned away. "Don't be long, okay?"

"I wish you wouldn't keep rushing me everywhere." She stepped into the bathroom and shut the door.

Ten minutes later she reappeared wearing a dress that clung to her body like a second skin.

"You look wonderful," Alex said in a voice caught between awe and disbelief.

"Thanks."

She stared at his dinner jacket and black trousers. He looked pretty damn desirable himself. "I don't know how I'll explain these last few days to my parents."

"Make something up." He ran a comb through his hair. "God knows I will."

"How can you lie to your own parents?"

"My family's interest in me these days is only marginal. Maybe I should have told you, I was adopted. Ever since I found out, I've never felt like I really belonged with them." He liked Jillian's pink compassionate gaze. Her sympathy was worth the lie. She was still evading too many questions and he needed her to open up fast. "Are you ready for the entertainment?"

Quickly, she brushed her hair. "What entertainment?"

"You'll see."

Jillian looked at him as she slipped into her black pumps. He really did look good. His golden strands of hair glowed at the tips and deepened into darker shades of rich, shining brown.

"Are you sure we should go out there?" she asked.

"No, but what the hell?"

At the door, Alex closed his eyes a moment, whispered something, then cautiously stepped into the corridor.

"Were you praying?" she asked softly.

"Thought we could use a little protection."

As they walked towards the end of the corridor, Alex looked at the oak doors with their brass numbers.

Jillian studied his pensive expression. "I like your gold cross."

"I inherited it from my grandmother. She and I went to church every Sunday. After she died I couldn't bring myself to go anymore."

At the end of the corridor, they stood in front of the set of doors they'd seen the couple enter earlier. Alex removed the plastic card from his pocket as he turned to her.

"You truly look lovely tonight."

"Thanks again. Quite the choice of dress. When did you find time to buy it?"

"I didn't. My friend bought it for you."

She tried to imagine who at the office had pictured her in something this glamorous. Which man knew her well enough to know the colour and size was absolutely right?

"Keep your eyes open," Alex said, "and if you recognize anyone, let me know. Also, watch for a short man with a damaged eye."

Jillian sighed. "Here we go again: cloak-and-dagger games with Sherlock Bond and his giant, garden-fresh cucumber."

Alex slipped the card in the slot. The door buzzed, they stepped inside, then clung to one another while trying to absorb the magnificence of this room.

It was as if all activity for miles around had been collected inside an enormous jewellery box. Sequins sparkled off mirrors and chandeliers. Laughter stretched in a room without end. People were clustered around craps, roulette, and blackjack tables enjoying loud, exuberant games while others chatted on sofas lining the two longer walls.

Stocky guys in navy blue suits stood around the perimeter of the room while handsome young men strolled amongst the players, chatting and occasionally disappearing, with female guests, through the doors on the other side of the casino. Beautiful young ladies in erotic evening gowns did the same with a variety of male guests. In a corner, at the far end of the casino, was a small enclosed area.

"That must be the bank," Alex stated. "Amazing, isn't it?"

"I think I just stumbled off the yellow brick road and walked straight into *The Twilight Zone*. How long has this casino been operating?"

"I don't know."

It couldn't have been long, he thought. A business like this was too dependent on the cooperation of the poorest guests, the largest losers, and the biggest mouths. If Barker operated continuously he'd increase his risk. If he operated infrequently, allowances would still have to be made for police raids and other break-ins. Alex wondered how quickly Barker could dismantle and refurbish this place, to turn his guests back into cribbage-playing vacationers.

At the far end of the room, a woman stepped out from a door in a wall made of one long mirror that extended as far as the bank.

Jillian's eyebrows shot up. "Did you see that?"

"Yeah." He led her further into the room. "Would you like to play a couple of hands?"

"What little cash I have is in our room."

"Don't worry, it's my treat. Wait here."

Jillian looked at the tables. The yellow chips were played most often, and she estimated their value at from two to five dollars. Chips not played were kept in handbags and pockets, making it difficult to distinguish winners from losers. If the furs and jewellery in this room were any indication, however, the money won wasn't as important as the way the game was played: illegally, defiantly, at the risk of losing something more valuable than cash.

A waiter handed Jillian a glass of champagne. Alex gave

her half-a-dozen yellow chips, plus two orange ones.

"Thanks. I'll pay you back."

"It's my treat. Blackjack brings you two and a half times your bet. Have you played before?"

"Las Vegas and Reno are my favourite escapes."

"Have a great time." He kissed her cheek and murmured, "If you do recognize anybody, try to make sure you're not seen."

"I'll hide in the bathroom, if I can find it."

"That's probably it." He pointed to two women stepping through a door in the mirror wall near their end of the room. A 'W' was painted on the glass.

"There's a poker room behind the mirrors next to the bank," he added.

"How do you know?"

"From Barker's response to the telegram from his wife. At her request, Tony faxed all sorts of detailed information to Mr. Reeves. I want to see what's happening with the poker. See you soon."

"Wait. Poker's my best game."

Her first boyfriend had taught her to play, which was how he'd managed to live on half of her pay cheques for six months, and why Jillian had worked at improving her game until she played better than he did.

"The room's for men only. There's a similar room for women around here somewhere, but I'd rather you didn't leave this area."

"So, I'm still a free person without options."

Alex kissed her forehead. "I know we're on our honeymoon, but I should tell you that two yellow chips or one orange one will buy you him for an hour." He nodded towards a tanned, Hollywood-type hunk standing nearby. "Just so you know that certain options are available."

She glanced at the man, then at the chips in her hand. "How much are these things worth?"

"Don't worry, he's cheap, although some of us don't

cost a penny."

"I thought you couldn't afford the distraction, or has this dress changed your mind?"

"Let's just say that I'm rethinking my options."

Jillian watched Alex disappear behind the glass, then took a closer look at the gigolo. He was gorgeous; broad shouldered and brown eyed; sleek, sexy, and stylish. He was a living romance novel hero: casual but not cold, distant but not impenetrable. He was cheap! Jillian tried to imagine what he'd look like in a tuxedo apron, until the man caught her gaze and smiled, as if the apron glowed warm in his pocket. She charged into the center of the blackjack area.

Tony's casino held the same range of playing skill as the Reno/Las Vegas crowds, yet the tension here was greater and some people seemed embarrassed to be watched. Others stared openly at Jillian, as if warning her not to look too hard because familiarity wasn't welcome here. Several players put a lot of energy into not looking at anything, while others gawked at every sparkle and gesture around them. And there were those dedicated souls unaware of anything but the game before them. They were the ones who glared at chips as if willing them to multiply, or who concentrated on each card with cold, analytic speculation.

Jillian chose a table where the players seemed fairly relaxed. Most of them smiled as she sat down and one older gentleman said, "Welcome to the poor man's table."

Laughing politely, she slapped a yellow chip down, but, as the rest of the table had warm bright colours stacked high, she added an orange chip to her bet. She slipped it carefully under the yellow one so both colours were visible. The dealer smiled patiently. He could afford to smile because he wasn't the one to place a hundred and fifty dollar bet at the poor man's table, she was.

♦ ♦ ♦

If it weren't for the thousands of dollars in chips stacked on table tops, the poker room would have resembled a cozy library. Crowded mahogany bookshelves filled the windowless room. Three doors were guarded by grim, beefy men who never took their eyes off the guests.

Alex strolled across the room to the bar. "Could I have a glass of orange juice, please?"

As the bartender placed the juice before him, Alex asked if Mr. Barker was available.

"He's in a blackjack game right now," he glanced at Alex, "in his private room."

"Is the table full?"

"There are special eligibility requirements."

"Yes, I know. My name is Reeves."

The bartender signalled to a man standing between two poker tables. As the man approached, Alex removed a small box from his pocket. He opened the box to display its contents. After examining the contents, the man picked up a telephone receiver and pressed two digits.

"Mr. Reeves wishes to join you. . . . Yes, he does. Everything's in order."

The man hung up, then nodded towards a far corner of the room. "Use that door. Our assistant will help you."

The assistant was a gigantic man with a face weather-beaten and porous and gritted with blackheads. He took a key from his pocket as a woman's voice said, "Barry?"

"Hi, Marlena," the assistant answered.

"Is Tony in there?"

"Yeah."

As casually as possible, Alex turned around. Marlena Margolin wore a shimmery black dress with a silver belt. The dress was cut low, the sleeves long and tight. Silver sparkles highlighted her bright pink eye-shadow. Her perfume was overbearing and sweet.

"Tell him to meet me in my suite the second he's free; it's important." She watched Alex sip his drink before she turned and strode out of the room.

Alex was guided into a room the size of a walk-in closet.

The door was shut and relocked. He wondered if Marlena had seen Jillian, if Jillian needed his help. As Alex considered turning back to see if he was needed, a wall slid away and Tony Barker stood there, poised and smiling serenely.

"Mr. Reeves." He shook Alex's hand. "Welcome."

"Thank you."

The man was exactly as Andy had described him: big, with electrifying blue eyes and a wide fringe of greyish white curls around his head. Barker escorted him into yet another room furnished with one blackjack table, two more exits, and an opulent collection of jewellery glittering inside display cases.

"The jewellery belongs to my wife," Barker explained. "There's nothing like a sixty-thousand-dollar necklace to revitalize fifty-year-old skin." He gazed at Alex. "How's my dear Sarah?"

Alex returned the smile, wary at the mention of Barker's wife. "Very well."

"We'll talk more later. I expect you'd like to try a little blackjack."

Alex gazed at the table. "I've never played with these stakes before."

"Few people have. Take a seat, Mr. Reeves, and enjoy."

Every man in the room stared at Alex. A thin, white-haired dealer shuffled the cards swiftly. Two solemn-looking men dressed in identical grey suits stood on either side of him. They studied Alex's face while Barker watched and waited.

As Alex sat down, the tension began to squeeze him. He was tempted to return the chair to Barker; however, the dealer's assistants had produced two trays for his perusal. Alex drank the orange juice to cool himself.

Dozens of cut and polished diamonds, rubies, emeralds, and sapphires sparkled from small compartments. The stones ranged from a carat in size up to four or five carats, or more.

Packed along the side of each tray were two rows of gold and silver wafers.

"I can only stay a minute." He turned to Tony.

"I understand."

Alex removed a silver wafer from his pocket and placed it on the table. The players looked away while the dealer's assistants glanced at Barker. The cards were swiftly dealt.

Alex stared at his ten and his queen. Aside from blackjack, twenty was the best hand he could have, yet he was afraid to put his cards down. The dealer had a ten showing. He flipped his second card over, exposed a jack — twenty-one: blackjack. The assistants swept everything away. Each player looked straight ahead, ignoring Alex completely.

He bet a second wafer and was grateful to be the only loser. Along the table, stones doubled as they were joined by comparable matches. The dealer's men moved with precision, their appraisal expertise allowing them to value the stones to within a fraction of a carat. When the transactions were completed, the man on Alex's right took two silver wafers from his pocket, and placed them in front of his diamonds. Silver was used to tip the dealer, Alex realized, and to inform newcomers that only rich men belonged in this room. He played a third wafer anyway, and won.

Soon everyone began winning and the players' jewels multiplied. Spotlights shone on every loose cluster until it seemed as if the table would ignite. Alex figured the size of these piles were designed partly to intimidate him, and although he was worried about Jillian, there was no leaving now, not without playing one big hand.

Alex pulled the box from his pocket, removed its lid and poked his finger at one emerald, one diamond, and one sapphire: three big hands. Tristan had had a good time buying the stones with Alex's money. He'd wanted to join them here, but Alex was afraid he'd be recognized.

For a half-second he wondered if someone in Special Investigations knew about this room. The casino had been so dazzling he'd forgotten to look for anyone with a damaged eye. Alex placed his emerald on the table and stared at it as his thoughts shrank and his senses poured energy into the stone. Suddenly, there was nothing except the desire to win. The dealer shuffled the cards soundlessly.

◆ ◆ ◆

Jillian was hiding in the women's room. She'd spotted Marlena moments after Alex's departure, then Alfred Lin had appeared. Jillian saw him speak to Marlena until Marlena signalled for one of those stocky security guard types in a blue suit and hurried towards the same mirrored wall Alex had entered. When Alfred had spotted the guard heading towards him, he'd quickly changed direction and merged with the crowd. As he'd moved closer to Jillian, she'd escaped to the bathroom before he could spot her. Now, she was afraid to leave. Since Alex wasn't likely to leap through the door and rescue her in the women's room, though, she knew she'd have to go find him.

Someone entered the room and walked towards the cubicles. There were six stalls altogether; Jillian was in the last one. As far as she could tell, none of the others were occupied, yet the woman stopped in front of her door. Jillian stood back to look at a skimpy pair of sandals with long spiked heels and a strap wound around the ankle. It was Marlena's style, all right. The door handle began to jiggle.

Jillian grumbled, "It's taken!" then flushed the toilet to prove it.

The jiggling stopped, then started again more forcefully. The woman pushed on the door as if determined to get inside. Jillian braced herself. She lifted her foot to kick the door back if it were opened.

Someone else entered the washroom, stopped, then turned around and left. The woman in spiked heels followed her out. Jillian waited until everything was quiet. Cautiously, she stepped out and was hurrying towards the exit when the door burst open and two giggling women brushed past her.

In the casino, she saw Marlena Margolin heading for the exit, then abruptly stopping. Jillian followed her gaze across the room and spotted the last person she wanted to see in this place.

Jerry Margolin was strolling amongst the guests and, judging by the way his eyes searched the room, looking for someone. As Marlena opened the door to the east corridor, Jerry spotted his wife and started towards her. Jillian wanted to stop Jerry, warn him to get out of here, but he was scowling and moving too fast. When he reached the exit, a security guard suddenly blocked his path. In an abrupt attempt to step around the guard, he bumped into another couple on their way out of the casino. The guard grabbed Jerry's arm to keep him from stumbling.

In the mirror, Jillian glanced at the reflected room. Seconds later, she discovered Les Silby staring at her. As he started his approach, Jillian side-stepped her way back to the women's room.

◆ ◆ ◆

Alex held twelve in his hand. The dealer had a ten showing and the men on his left had placed their cards face down.

The player on the far right signalled for a card, received a ten and lost on twenty-four. The player next to Alex also signalled for a card, received a five, and placed his cards down. It was Alex's turn.

Alex wanted another card badly, but ten or a face card would put him over twenty-one and he'd lose his emerald. He played the hand as it was and waited.

The dealer flipped his second card over. It was three, bringing his total to thirteen. He drew another card: a two, for a total of fifteen. As the house rules did not allow a dealer to stop before seventeen, he dealt himself another card — a Queen for twenty-five, and Alex was given an emerald identical to his own. The other players glanced at his cards, then nodded at Alex, acknowledging a well-played hand. Alex quickly slipped one of the emeralds into his pocket.

The cards were dealt and Alex had blackjack. He was paid with two more emeralds and a fairly large sapphire. Next, he was dealt eighteen and stayed. The dealer had nineteen. As Alex's bet was swept away, he stood up, thanked his host and was escorted to the alcove. Tony pushed a button, the wall slid back, and when the guard opened the door, Alex darted out.

He spotted Jillian behind a rubber plant on the other side of the room. She beckoned Alex over. Smiling, he beckoned back and tried not to laugh as she walked stiffly towards him.

"What took you so long?" She smacked his arm.

"There was a lot going on in there."

"There was a hell of a lot going on out here, too! I think Marlena saw me."

She told him about Alfred and Marlena's conversation and the episode in the bathroom.

"Is Alfred still here?" Alex glanced at faces. He searched for a man with a damaged eye, someone perhaps wearing glasses. If the guy had needed the pair he lost in Silby & Morrow's stairwell, then he probably still needed to wear glasses.

"I don't know. I only saw Alfred once," she answered. "I watched Marlena send a security guard after him, but Alfred was trying to avoid the guard, so maybe he's still around somewhere."

Alex took Jillian's hand and they headed for the exit. "What would Alfred want with Mrs. Margolin?"

"They know each other." Her answer was more sarcastic than she intended.

"Are they having an affair?"

Tristan had heard rumours around the office.

"She and Jerry have only been married a few months, Alex."

Leaving the casino, Alex and Jillian hurried down the

hall of the mansion's east wing until Alex suddenly stopped and let go of her hand. He turned around and walked back to a suite they had just passed on the right-hand side of the hall.

"What is it?" she whispered.

The door was open just a little. He listened. No sound came from the room. Alex tried to peer inside, but only a wall was visible.

He knocked on the door, opening it further. There was still no sound from the suite. Alex pushed the door open wider until he saw a woman resting on a sofa. Her head was turned away from him. He spun around and looked at Jillian. The smell of blood and feces and urine overpowered the woman's familiar perfume. In a flash, he was back in Andy's apartment, gagging on the smell of death.

"Stay out here." Alex took a long deep breath. Slowly, reluctantly, he stepped inside.

He peered at Marlena Margolin's dark red hair and her beautiful black dress. Her wrists were sliced open, her hands resting in her blood-soaked lap. More blood seeped into the upholstery and trickled down her black stockings, making the butterfly designs on each ankle look like engorged mosquitos. It slid over her feet and into her silver shoes, onto the carpet. Alex stepped closer.

He looked for wounds to her head and hands, but saw no signs of a struggle. Had she known her assailant? Alex stared at her open mouth; her fixed and dilated pupils. A diamond and pearl choker sparkled against her throat.

Jillian made a sound, collapsed on the floor behind him and started to retch. Alex helped her up, checked the hallway, and rushed her into their own suite three doors down and across the hall.

"Will you be okay?" He sat her on the sofa. "We've got to get out of here. The killer probably saw us in the casino."

"Poor Marlena," she murmured. "Poor Jerry."

"Is he here?"

"Yes." Jillian stumbled to the bathroom.

Alex thought of the open door to Marlena's suite. Was it carelessness on the killer's part, or was she supposed to have been found quickly? She'd been dead a very short time, which meant her killer had either just left, or he'd been hiding in the room. Alex stared at the door, then ran to the bedroom and tossed their suitcase onto the bed.

"Time to leave." He started to pack: rushing, dumping, snapping the suitcase shut while Jillian came out of the bathroom and sat down, shaken and dazed. He helped her into her grey cardigan, watched her try to comprehend what she'd seen.

"Alex?" She drew her knees up, wrapped her arms around her legs and began to rock back and forth. "Les was also in the casino."

He sat next to her. "When?"

"The same time Jerry and Marlena were."

"What happened?"

"I don't know." She stared at the suitcase. "When he saw me, I hid in the bathroom."

"Did Marlena speak to Jerry?"

"Not when I saw them." Jillian kept rocking as she described Jerry's attempt to follow Marlena out of the casino.

Alex said, "Did anyone else follow her out?"

"Another couple, I think, but then I saw Les. By the time I stepped outside again everyone was gone."

"Did you recognize the couple?"

"No. They had their backs to me."

Someone knocked on the door.

Alex and Jillian looked at one another. He wrapped his arms around her. There was a second knock, louder, more insistent. When all was quiet again Alex tiptoed to the door. He couldn't hear anything in the hallway. He looked through the keyhole; spotted the door across the hall. He touched the handle, then changed his mind. He watched a little longer and tried the handle again. The door opened. He peered into the corridor. No one was there.

"Okay, bring the suitcase and let's go."

Jillian shook her head.

"Why not?"

"She was right." Her wide, unblinking eyes were riveted on the door. "It's too dangerous outside."

"Who was right?"

Jillian kept staring at the door.

"Come on!" Alex hurried over and grabbed her arm. "Move!"

They ran down the east wing of the estate, their footsteps pounding on the carpet. Alex heard noises coming from the casino, then all was quiet again. Someone was behind them. He turned around and saw an elderly couple enter a suite.

He and Jillian jogged down the empty north wing as another door opened behind them. Without looking back, they bolted down the stairs, across the panelled foyer and onto the porch outside. Together, they ran down the steps towards the gate. While Alex was inserting his card in the slot, the lodge door flew open. He spun around.

A man was silhouetted in the light. He was smaller than the guy who'd let them in, too short to be either Les Silby or Tony Barker. The man hurried down the steps after them.

"Jillian, how tall is Jerry Margolin?"

"About five foot five: why?"

As the gate opened, Alex began to run. He imagined cold hands on the back of his neck; pale, small, and razor sharp. Alex stumbled, dropping the suitcase. Jillian turned to help him and saw the man running towards them.

"Alex!"

"Let's go!" They charged down the wooden steps onto the pier. By the time they reached the boat the man had disappeared. Alex jumped in the boat and reached for Jillian as she looked at the steps.

"Jillian, move!"

"We've got to get the suitcase."

"Get in the boat!"

"If we leave it behind, Tony will find out who we are."

"He'll find out anyway. Get in!"

"My diary's in there! I've been making notes about the partners and the things we've talked about. Thought it would help me remember something."

"Oh, God."

"Fine, I'll go myself."

"Wait!" He removed the pistol he'd hidden under a pile of rope, then scrambled onto the pier.

"Stay here, damn it!"

Alex charged up the stairs. He looked at the bushes and listened for sounds. He crept further down the path, half-surprised to find the suitcase still there. He leaned over to pick it up.

Jillian climbed the first six steps, wanting to go after him, yet afraid to leave the lights of the pier. Hugging herself, she rocked back and forth on her heels. Something moved in the bushes to her right. Jillian peered into the blackness.

"Alex, is that you?" Nothing moved. "If this is a joke, you can stop any time." She waited a few moments. "I'll go home without you. I'm going now."

Jillian started back down the stairs as a man wearing a blue and red ski mask stepped out of the darkness.

She screamed, then raced down the steps and onto the pier. She heard him follow close behind, felt a hand clamp down on her shoulder and fingers dig into her skin. Wrenching herself from his grasp, Jillian started to run but he grabbed the back of her cardigan. The man pulled hard. Jillian twisted back and forth. She slipped the cardigan off her shoulders and yanked her arms free. The man went for her, grabbing one arm, then bending it behind her back. In the pier's lights, a razor blade appeared in front of her face. Jillian screamed again and turned her head. The blade slashed her hair.

Alex reached the pier. He fired a shot in the air. As the

man turned around, Jillian elbowed him with all her strength. The blade fell on the ground. He pushed Jillian into the water, pulled off his mask, then jumped in after her.

Alex wanted to shoot again but their bodies were entwined and struggling. He leaned over the pier, then jumped back. He gasped for breath and leaned forward again, swinging his arms as if preparing to dive in. He saw himself underneath the upside-down canoe, scrambling to get out. Alex opened his mouth wide, as if to shout, then breathed deeply. Again he stepped back and watched in horror as the attacker pushed Jillian's head underwater.

He shouted, "No!"

Jillian clutched her attacker, and pulled him down with her. Feet and arms thrashed; they struggled to the surface and gasped for air.

Alex fired a shot just above them, saw the man break free and vanish between the boats.

Jillian swam to the edge of the pier and, when she could breathe again, glared up at him. "You could have shot me!"

"I made sure to aim high above you."

He helped her onto the pier, then looked at the water. Jillian's assailant was nowhere in sight.

She picked up the face mask and dangled it in front of Alex. Splotches of dried blood covered a large part of the mask. "I take it this is familiar to you?"

He nodded. "Did you see his face?"

"I was too busy to get a good look, Alex." She dropped the mask and stared at the bloodstained eye holes. "His right eye was damaged or deformed, or something. I guess that lets Jerry out."

A gust of wind chilled the back of Alex's neck. "You haven't seen him lately."

"It wasn't him; the eyebrows weren't right. Jerry's are long and tapered, and this guy had fuzzy straight things like caterpillars. He also looked older."

"I thought you didn't see his face."

"That's all I saw. It wasn't Jerry."

Which didn't actually prove his innocence in Marlena's death, Alex thought. It could have been a joint effort: one holding her down, the other slicing her wrists open . . . two killers. Also, the man in the stairwell at Silby & Morrow had worn glasses, while his assailant in the parking lot hadn't worn any. Alex recalled the man's filmy blue-grey eyes blinking at him from behind the mask; a man struggling to see? Jillian's assailant hadn't been wearing glasses either, yet his eye had been damaged. Was there one killer after all? One shadow following them?

He bent down to pick up Jillian's cardigan. A tissue fell out of the pocket. "Let's go before the bastard comes back."

He tossed the suitcase in the boat, helped Jillian in, started the engine and sped away from the dock. He wanted to ask Jillian more about Jerry Margolin but she was busy removing her wet clothes. She took one of Alex's shirts out of the suitcase and, keeping her back to him, began to dry herself. Casually, he stepped to one side and watched his shirt glide over her breasts, then down her stomach and over her backside. He gasped when the shirt slipped between her legs.

"I was going to wear that." He swallowed hard.

Jillian put on a yellow pullover. "Shouldn't you be steering the damn boat?"

"What did you mean when you said, 'she was right'?"

"When did I say that?"

"Just before we left the suite."

"I told you, my mother's agoraphobic. She thinks nothing's safe outside. I'd started to think she was right."

Alex spotted a boat speeding after them.

When she was dressed, Jillian watched the water churn into slabs of black and white marble. The patterns reminded her of the marble in the bathroom at the casino. She thought of Jerry trying to catch up with his wife in the casino, and of Alfred Lin's chat with Marlena. She hugged herself and tried not to shake.

"Stand by me to warm up." Alex reached for her.

He glanced behind him and also began to tremble. The boat was only a few yards away and gaining.

TWENTY-FOUR

In the restaurant, Les and Isobel grew increasingly irritated with Craig and Martin's bickering. What was supposed to have been a quiet meal for two had somehow been interpreted as an open invitation to a partners' lunch.

"You don't know what you're talking about." Martin glared at Craig. "The rich are the productive element in society and anyone earning under sixty thousand dollars a year is a burden on the rest. Tristan Wells is a perfect example."

"There's nothing wrong with Tristan." Craig poured his fourth glass of wine. He'd been drinking for two hours, trying to forget the divorce papers he'd been served with this morning. "We've got plenty of good staff."

"Plenty of partners, anyway," Martin muttered.

Craig smacked his lips and smiled at Les. "Which reminds me, when's Jillian coming back?"

Martin stabbed his salad. The line between his eyebrows turned purple.

"She is okay, isn't she, Les?" Isobel asked. "You look so worried."

Les wiped his hands on a serviette. "I'd feel better if I knew where each of you was yesterday afternoon. I had hoped to call a quick meeting to discuss several other clients who've been neglected lately, but most of you had apparently left for the day."

No one answered. Isobel lit a cigarette and observed Les closely.

"I was with a client." Craig scribbled a phone number on his serviette. "Check it out."

"It's not necessary."

"I just want to give you a little peace of mind, Les."

"Then stop drinking!"

Craig's wine glass hovered in midair.

"Les doesn't trust us anymore. He can't understand why we don't handle problems the way he does." Craig looked at the pill bottle beside Martin's glass. "Of course, he trusts Jillian and Jerry, though I don't know why since they've both disappeared. Who knows? Maybe there's something about Les we shouldn't trust."

Martin moved the pills closer to his plate. "Leslie knows where I was yesterday."

"Did the doctor spend an entire afternoon on you?" Craig smiled slyly, then looked at Isobel. "And where was Ms. Cameron on the afternoon in question?"

"In and out," she answered abruptly.

"Your appointment book was empty; I checked," Craig stated. "Your secretary said you were taking care of family business."

"I heard it was a client meeting." Martin stared at Isobel.

"Oh!" Craig clapped his hands together. "Caught in a lie. It must have been a lover's tryst. Not with a married man, I hope. You do have that haggard, abandoned look about you."

His wife had worn the same look the last time he saw her. Craig leered at Isobel, convinced that sex with her would be intriguing.

"The client meeting's this afternoon." Isobel tore open a bread roll. "I won't be back today."

"You're kicking him out!" Craig slapped the table, hitting the edge of his side plate. "Good for you. You single career women have everything. Why ruin it on married men?

They're just shit piles with shrivelling organs." Or so he'd confessed to his wife over the phone this morning. Liz hadn't been moved by his emotional outburst, and the first tears he'd ever produced for her had been wasted.

"That is disgusting!" Martin dropped his fork.

"It's also not true," Isobel said, "because Craig thinks with his cock and keeps pissing on himself, which no doubt keeps his brain nice and supple."

"This is what we get for having a female partner!" Martin watched Les throw ten dollars down on the table, then get up and leave the restaurant.

An eight-block drive later, he turned into the underground parking lot of his office building. Shutting the motor off, Les tried to get out of the car but found his door blocked. Alex was holding the handle.

"Stay there." He hurried to the passenger side and slid in beside Les.

"Where's Jillian?" Les asked. "Is she all right?"

"She's fine."

"Why aren't you with her?"

"She's sleeping in the car right over there." Alex pointed to the row of vehicles ahead of them. He'd chosen his parking spot carefully, and turned to examine Les's reaction.

"I want her back today, Alex."

"Soon, but not yet." He glanced at the cars behind him.

"Why the hell not?"

As Alex told him about Marlena's death on Barker's island the night before, Les's shoulders sagged.

"I knew she'd died, but I didn't know how, until now."

"Did you know Marlena well, Les?"

"Yes and no. Barker introduced her to Jerry. Jerry fell in love with her and wound up working seven days a week to keep Revenue Canada off Barker's back. I don't know why she was killed."

Alex listened for sounds in the parking lot. "Did Jerry go to the island with her often?"

"Yesterday was his first visit." Les stared at him. "He didn't kill his wife."

"How can you be sure?"

His gaze became hostile. "You'd better look after Jillian."

"She's safe, Les, believe me. No one's going to harm our sweet lady."

"Which car is she in?"

Alex watched him closely. "Is it important?"

"Do you have some objection to telling me?"

"I don't want you to wake her. She had a lousy night's sleep."

Les stared at him, then swiftly reached for the glove box. "I have something for you." He removed the broken eye-glasses.

Alex froze as he looked for a weapon in the compartment. If Les was innocent of any crime, then why wasn't he revealing that he'd visited the island last night? Alex examined the glasses. The right lens was gone. He removed his own glasses, then carefully put the broken pair on and looked at Les through the left lens. The lens wasn't strong. The owner could probably get by without them for a short while.

"Do your partners know about Barker's island?"

"Why do you ask?" One of the cars caught Les's attention: a Volvo parked on a slight angle, as if the driver had been in a hurry.

"I need information, Les. Anything you can tell me about their whereabouts, activities, or acquaintances over recent weeks could help."

"I persuaded Jerry to go with me to Barker's island." He paused. "Unfortunately, Alfred Lin was there, to get something from Marlena, he said."

Alex took a deep breath, then let it out slowly. "Did Jerry talk with his wife?"

"No. We were both in the casino when he spotted her as

she was about to leave. He followed her until a rather large man stopped him at the door."

"Did Jerry say why he was stopped?"

"The man was an employee who wanted to know who Jerry was and why he was rushing."

"Did you see anyone else follow Marlena out of the casino?"

"Just one other couple."

"Anyone you recognized?"

"I only saw the back of them as they were leaving. Then I noticed Jillian and went to talk to her, but she managed to avoid me."

Alex glanced around the parking lot. This wasn't the safest place to be chatting with a potential enemy. Casually, he reached into his jacket pocket. His fingertips touched the pistol.

"When I left the casino, I saw you and Jillian enter a room," Les announced. "When I knocked on the door, you wouldn't answer."

"We were too scared. We'd just found Marlena's body in a suite across the hall, three doors down from ours."

Les lowered his eyes.

"How did Alfred know about the island, Les?"

"He didn't until Sam Roche raised the subject. We talked about it after Jerry told me what he knew about the place."

"Did you tell Alfred how to find the island?"

Les hesitated. "I'm sorry I did."

"What did Alfred want to get from Marlena?"

"Photographs of some sort. When I saw him in Barker's casino, I suggested he leave because Jerry was also there."

Alex frowned.

"I've known Alfred a long time." Les watched him. "He has a temper but he's never gone over the edge. He'd have no reason to kill Sam. The man was fired and was about to face criminal charges anyway, and Marlena was certainly no threat to him."

"Why did he go to the island to get pictures from her, and how did he know she'd even be there?"

"I don't know."

"Where is Jerry now?"

"Home, I suppose. After I gave up waiting for Jillian to reappear, from what presumably was the washroom, I decided to catch up with Jerry, but he'd also vanished. I searched every room I had access to, before I found him back in the casino two hours later, pale and shaken. He said his wife was dead, but he wouldn't say how or why. In fact, he didn't speak the entire way home. The poor man's probably still in shock."

Les rubbed his eyes. "Barker could have killed her. Look what he's doing on the bloody island! I knew that man was trouble, damn him!"

"Did all your partners show up for work this morning?"

A car engine turned over. Alex glanced around the parking lot.

"Obviously, Jerry didn't." He looked at Alex slowly. "Which car is Jillian in?"

"Red Mustang. I guess you don't know where the rest of your partners were last night."

"I made enquiries," he answered coolly. "According to Mrs. Sloane, Martin was in bed by eight. Craig and Isobel weren't answering their phones."

"I admire your efficiency."

"What efficiency? If I'd been on top of things the firm wouldn't be in this mess now, and if I don't take steps to get rid of certain problems in my office, I'll wind up like Alfred." He looked at the cars ahead. "You said she's in the red Mustang?"

"Yes." Alex scanned the parking lot for possible allies or witnesses, should Les suddenly turn on him.

He couldn't help wondering if Les was somehow responsible for recent events. Was his dislike for Barker an act to disguise a profitable working relationship? Perhaps all the conspirators had met on the island to tie up loose ends.

"I'd like to talk to Jillian," Les said quietly, "say hello."

"She's had a rough night," Alex answered. "If she was awake, she'd sit up."

"Knowing her, she'd get out of the car, head upstairs, and start working. It'll be good to have her back."

"What if she doesn't want to come back?"

Les stared at him. "All right, what have you done?"

"Nothing."

"You've said something to influence her against us?"

"I swear, I haven't. Jillian hasn't said a word about quitting."

"Then she'll be back?"

"I'm sure of it." Alex opened the door. "Take care."

He walked around the back of the car, then disappeared behind a cement partition on Les's left. Les stepped out of his car and began to approach the Mustang.

Alex emerged from behind the partition. His hand reached for the gun in his pocket. Ten feet away, Les stopped, turned and stared at him, then headed for the elevators. In his office, he dialled Jerry Margolin's number.

"Jerry?" Les rested his elbows on the desk. "I just called to see if you're all right, and if there's anything I can do."

The garbled reply sounded shaky and weak.

"Do you want me to come over?"

"No . . . Tony's bringing Marlena home today. I've got to go." Jerry hung up.

Les's face burned as Tristan bounded into his office. "I've almost completed the bank proposal for Alfred. Do you want to see a rough draft? It's pretty good."

"It should have been on my desk before lunch."

"I was helping one of the newer students with a problem."

"Personal or professional?"

"It was kind of personal. Women troubles."

The boy was all pink-faced innocence. Les scowled as he thought about innocence and fear; his freedom and Jillian's, splashed like stains on a clean white canvas.

"Is something wrong?" Tristan asked.

"Yes. Your priorities." He stared at him. "Which is why I'm firing you. Clean out your desk today."

As Tristan turned around and quickly left the room, Les thought about all the deadlines that young man had missed because of personal issues and a complete lack of discipline. This firm needed to get back on track, to run efficiently again.

The telephone rang and Martin's shrill voice bellowed over the noise of the restaurant.

"Craig lied about being with a client yesterday afternoon. He was in one of those disgusting hotels."

"I know he lied."

"Oh, well, that's just marvellous. Why didn't you say something?"

The phone call Les had had from Craig's client demanding an explanation for his partner's absence, wasn't an issue he'd wanted to discuss in the restaurant.

"I'm waiting until after lunch."

"Considering how much alcohol he's had, and that it's nearly three o'clock, I doubt if he'll be back from lunch. Honestly, Leslie, you shouldn't schedule such late lunches."

"I left the restaurant at 2:15," he retorted. "Why are you still there?"

"Someone has to make sure he doesn't do something stupid. By the way, I'm going to tell him that you know about his lie." He hung up.

Les removed his glasses, closed his eyes, and wondered how Martin knew Craig had lied. He placed his head in his hands and remained that way as the phone rang again.

TWENTY-FIVE

"Jillian," Alex said, and peered at her, "you can sit up now."

"I like it down here."

She was curled up in the back seat half-asleep, her voice muffled under the blanket. They'd spent a restless night at a motel in Sechelt, waiting to catch the ferry at Langdale this morning.

As soon as they'd reached the shore last night, their nemesis had turned his boat around and sped back toward the island. As they'd driven through Vancouver this morning, Alex had realized they were being followed. The creep must have been on the same ferry.

They'd lost the guy by pulling into a police station and heading inside, though not too far inside. About then, Alex had begun to wonder if Jillian's presence could evoke a response from Les, something which might reveal his guilt or innocence in the fraud, and maybe gain him some insight into whether Jerry Margolin was also involved.

After asking Tristan to check Les's schedule, Alex had decided to confront Les on his way back from lunch. Unfortunately, the man had given nothing away. Any partner could still be guilty of murder, and he was no further ahead than he had been the night Andy died. Alex smacked the steering wheel.

"Jillian, help me."

"How?" she mumbled.

"I still don't know who's trying to kill us."

"You could always drive back to the police station and actually talk to somebody this time." She peeked out from under the blanket. "Considering everything we saw and went through last night, I don't understand why you won't get help."

"They'd arrest me for theft and kidnapping. I've also been at two murder scenes. How do you think they'll treat me when that news comes out, and who will protect you when I'm locked up?"

"Why would you be charged with theft?"

He repeated Ida Gowan's comments about Revenue Canada's anxiousness to get back their files.

"So, if I'm to come out of this in one piece, I need you to tell me more about the Thursday your anonymous calls started. Specifically, I'd like to know what the partners were up to that day."

She started to sneeze.

"Oh, great. Here comes the cold." She sneezed again. "I hate this, Alex."

"Jillian, I need your cooperation! The killer isn't far away!"

She sneezed again. "Oh, God."

"When will you stop playing games with me?"

"Playing games with you? PLAYING GAMES WITH YOU!" She sat up. "Who's been running around playing hide-and-seek with everybody? Who's been jeopardizing other peoples' lives so he can beat the bad guys, because if there's one thing Alex Bellamy hates, it's losing, which is why he thinks I should cooperate, and why a murderer should surrender to a thoughtless, self-serving, Revenue Canada auditor!"

"Poor Jillian also hates being pulled out of her dull comfy routine but never mind, you worry about your cold while the killer goes free."

He started the car as Jillian climbed over the front seat and flopped down beside him.

"I'm sorry, Alex, but I'm exhausted and running low on patience."

He gazed at her. "All of the partners stayed late that Thursday night, right?"

She leaned against the headrest and sighed. "Craig left first: between eight and nine, I think."

Alex glanced around the parking lot. The car that had followed them this morning was mid-sized and beige-coloured.

"How late did Martin Sloane stay?"

"I don't know. He was unhappy about something and wanted to see Les, but Les was on the phone for ages, so he gave up and disappeared."

"What was Isobel Cameron up to that night?"

"Trying to send a fax when I saw her." Jillian leaned towards him. "I also saw Tony Barker standing in the reception area alone. He shouldn't have been able to get in because I'd already shut the elevators off, and the stairwell door is permanently locked," she said, then hesitated, "unless someone gave him a key."

"You think Jerry might have?"

"Maybe. The partners and senior staff have keys, so Barker could have gotten it from a number of people."

"Then it doesn't prove anything."

She folded her arms. "I'm trying, Alex."

"What happened next?"

"Nothing. I left shortly after their meeting started."

Alex brushed his hand through his hair. "You must be missing something. Were all the partners there when Barker arrived?"

"Craig had gone home by then."

"Unless he wanted everyone to think he'd gone home."

Jillian looked at him. "There's something else I should tell you."

"I'm listening."

"Earlier that night I overheard Martin tell Craig that this year's Lions Imports financial statements had better be right. He said he had no intention of letting Craig put the firm at risk over sloppy audit work."

Alex removed his glasses. "Martin knew something was wrong with the numbers?"

"Not necessarily. He's always lecturing Craig about his work."

"What did Craig say?"

"I couldn't hear, but I imagine it wasn't nice."

Alex put his glasses back on. "Did either of them know you'd overheard their conversation?"

"I don't think so. Anyway, I left for the file room." She paused. "When we were in Tony's suite and you asked me which partner I thought was guilty, a name did come to mind."

"Craig McBride?"

She nodded. "He's been making a lot of mistakes lately and Les has been riding him hard, taking some of his responsibilities away."

Alex frowned. "That doesn't sound good."

"It's not, and there's been resentment on both sides. I'm not sure Les is aware of the effect he's had on people."

"Maybe he knows and doesn't care."

"I think he cares so much he can't imagine harming the firm."

"What happened after Martin and Craig's conversation?"

"Nothing. I went to the file room and showed Isobel how to unjam the fax machine."

"How long were you there?"

"A few minutes. The machine ate her memo every time she tried to send it. I offered to retype the whole thing because the paper was a mess and she'd made a couple of typing errors anyway, but she was way too stressed out to wait."

Leaning against the headrest, Alex closed his eyes. "I thought Isobel was the calm, controlled type."

"She usually is. I think I startled her by showing up in the file room in the first place, and I don't think she appreciated me pointing out the typos, but changing RC to IC was no big deal. I wouldn't have minded doing it. It was the first time she'd really been annoyed with me."

Alex opened his eyes. RC was Revenue Canada abbreviated; he'd written it a thousand times. "What do you mean, RC to IC?"

"Isobel's initials are IC but she'd typed RC instead. In fact, she mixed up those two letters a couple of times, but she was pretty tired that night."

"Does she normally type her own memos?"

"After hours, yes. Her secretary's a single parent who can't stay late."

"Jillian," Alex tried to sound casual, "did you see who she was sending the fax to?"

She narrowed her eyes. "Why?"

"Let's see how good your memory is." His smile was brief.

"What for?"

"Humour me."

"The fax was addressed to a woman, I think."

"Really?"

"No, it could have been a man or woman. The name was Terry, or Kerry or something." She reached in her sleeve for a tissue. "Kelly! That's it."

"What was the last name?"

Jillian fumbled with her sweater sleeves. "Faust." She spelled it out for him.

RC: Revenue Canada . . . Kelly Faust. The name was familiar. Alex didn't think there'd been any typing mistake. His heart began to race. "What did the fax say?"

Jillian stared at him. "Why are you so interested?"

"Because I keep hearing about your perfect memory and

I have twenty bucks that says it isn't perfect."

"It was just a simple little memo. On the first line, she'd typed, 'RC dash Kelly Faust'. On the second line, she'd typed, 'IC audit underway.'"

Alex waited. "Go on."

"That's all I saw."

He gazed at her. "What did those two lines mean?"

"First of all, she was using our memo format. The top line was supposed to read, 'IC dash Kelly Faust', which meant from Isobel Cameron to Kelly Faust. Are you with me so far?"

"I'm managing."

"On the second line, where she said IC, it should have been RC. Isobel was telling Mr. Faust that an audit of his company was about to start. Some clients panic over stuff like that." She gazed at Alex. "If you're the auditor I can understand why."

"She said Kelly Faust was a client?"

"I think so." Jillian opened the car door. "Want me to go upstairs and confirm it?"

Alex pulled her back. "Shut the door."

"Swine."

If there hadn't been any typing errors, the message made perfect sense. IC was Ice Craft; the message was to Kelly Faust at Revenue Canada, telling him Ice Craft was being audited. She could have known about the audit before Faust did. It wouldn't be difficult for a partner at a small accounting firm to keep track of audits. Alex clasped his hands together and tried to stay calm.

"Was the phone number local?"

"Yes."

"If Isobel was making typing mistakes and having trouble with the fax machine, why wouldn't she just have phoned the client?"

"I asked her that. She said she'd tried to reach the guy for hours, and since she had to be on an early flight to

Calgary the next morning, she wouldn't have time to call him."

"Jillian, do all your partners know Jerry's wife?"

"Yeah, why?" She watched him closely. "Alex, what's wrong?"

"In the casino you said you knew Marlena was on the other side of the bathroom door because of the style of shoes she'd been wearing."

"That's right."

"What were those shoes like?"

"They were skimpy black sandals with an ankle strap."

"Black sandals?"

"Yes." Jillian studied his face. "What's going on?"

Alex clearly remembered blood seeping into Marlena's silver shoes. Had it been Isobel trying to get to Jillian when Marlena entered the washroom? If she'd been in the casino, surely Les would have recognized her, though. Had he missed Isobel, or had he not wanted anyone to know he'd seen her? Both Les and Jillian had mentioned that a couple followed Marlena out of the casino. A partnership — Isobel and Les Silby? Jerry Margolin? Kelly Faust? Alex kept his eyes straight ahead, refusing, absolutely, to panic.

"Alex, what aren't you telling me?"

"Marlena wouldn't have wanted her voice recognized." He turned to Jillian. "That's why she didn't say anything to you in the bathroom."

He started the car. "How would you like a hot bath and some sleep?"

She buckled her seat belt. "Take me to it."

It was three o'clock now, which would give him enough time to drop her off at the Beach Avenue apartment, then drive to West Pender Street and hide inside Revenue Canada until everyone went home.

TWENTY-SIX

Alex screeched to a halt in front of the apartment building, eager to keep moving. He envisioned every inch of the floor he worked on at Revenue Canada, and planned where he would hide once inside. He knew how long it would take most people to leave the premises for the day. He also knew where Special Investigations was located and where he might find Kelly Faust's office, but this was as far as his plan went. Andy was the one who'd always worked out the details and considered a problem from all angles.

Somehow, he had to get evidence of Faust's part in the fraud, then get the hell out before anyone saw him. Alex didn't want Jillian anywhere near Faust's territory. Jillian, however, didn't want to be anywhere else.

"Come on, Bellamy, you dragged me into this. Why can't I go?"

"You need some sleep, and I may be a while."

"What's at Revenue Canada?"

"A couple of files to examine." Alex squeezed her hand. "Don't worry, I've got everything worked out, sort of."

She gave him a bleak, unforgiving look.

"I'll call you when I get to the office."

"I'll be far too busy snooping through your apartment to answer the phone. I'm going through every drawer, Alex, because you went through everything at my place."

"You can't look around; the apartment's not mine. It

belongs to a friend."

Jillian stared at him. "I don't believe you."

"Since the killer knew where Andy lived, I figured he knew at least that much about me. Why do you think we were in a tunnel to begin with?"

"Why did you want me to think you lived here?"

Alex pulled a set of keys from his pocket. "My friend needs anonymity to stay safe."

Jillian took the keys from Alex.

"I'll take you upstairs," he said.

"I can manage, thanks."

She retrieved the suitcase from the back seat and headed into the building. When she was inside, Alex pulled away from the curb. In his haste, he didn't see Kelly Faust watching and waiting just three cars back.

TWENTY-SEVEN

Jillian put her suitcase down. She looked around the room and wondered who all this hi-tech tranquility belonged to, and whether she should snoop or not.

From the window, the world below seemed gentle and sedate; far removed from the craziness she'd experienced with Alex. Her relationship with him would end soon, find her back at home folding laundry with the television on for company.

Jillian studied the decor of the room. She resented how much Alex had kept from her, how he'd gone through her apartment without permission and, despite what he said, she intended to snoop a little.

As she approached the master bedroom, Isobel Cameron walked out, carrying a set of financial statements.

"Isobel!" Jillian stared at her, then blushed. "Oh my God, is this your apartment?"

Isobel stared back at her and swiftly shut the bedroom door. "I wasn't expecting anyone this soon."

"Alex said his friend was a man. Alex also lies a lot. I'm sorry for barging in on you."

Isobel smiled briefly. "Please, sit down."

"I thought you had a house in Burnaby."

"I did." She sat in a chair opposite Jillian, placed the statements on her lap, and her handbag on top of the statements. "Where is Alex now?"

"On his way to Revenue Canada."

Isobel's hands shook as she lit a cigarette. Strands of dark blonde hair had slipped out of her braid.

"Are you okay?"

She dropped the cigarette pack in her purse, then observed Jillian closely. "Is Alex going to see Kelly Faust?"

Jillian paused. "He said he wanted to look at files." She frowned slightly. "Why do you ask?"

Isobel flicked ashes onto a coaster. "It's part of man's nature to keep secrets from women, certainly part of his perversity."

Jillian nodded. "I know what you mean."

"I'm sure you do." Isobel watched her closely. "Women who watch other women struggle in a man's world see their discontentment; still, you should pay more attention to causes, Jillian."

Jillian was unnerved by the severity of Isobel's voice, and as she watched her, a new understanding began to emerge; an answer as disturbing as the confrontation between herself and a woman on the other side of a bathroom door; a woman desperate to break in and force both of them to face the truth.

Sweat burst over Jillian. She pressed her back against the sofa and stared at Isobel through the slow bright burn on her face.

"Does Kelly Faust work in Revenue Canada's Special Investigations Division, by any chance?"

Isobel slowly nodded.

Jillian's temples began to throb. She slumped against the sofa.

"I remembered the obscene phone calls you had last summer," Isobel said, and glanced down at her open handbag, "and had hoped a similar situation, especially one that invaded your office, would upset you enough to make you quit your job."

Jillian's voice was subdued. "Why did you hurt the

firm?"

Embers glowed as Isobel sucked on her cigarette, then exhaled slowly. "I could put up with Craig's and Martin's demoralizing confrontations, their attempts to embarrass me in front of clients, even Craig's silly efforts to sabotage my work."

"Sabotage?"

"He changed the numbers on a couple of clients' financial statements. At first he denied it, then he said the whole thing was a joke. Students were blamed for the third episode, but Craig and I knew better. Anyway, the last straw came when he showed up at my house one night, looking for sex."

"When was this?"

"A few months ago. The bastard was drunk. Smashed a window and tried to climb in." She mashed the cigarette butt into the coaster. "Later, he started threatening to return, armed and well prepared."

Jillian remembered Craig's remark to Isobel near the elevators on her last morning at the office: something about bringing burglary tools.

"By itself, the incident wasn't important," Isobel said, "but I realized that no matter what I did for the firm, or how hard I worked, nothing would change. In fact, I figured things would only get worse. That's when I decided on a little revenge."

"I'm almost afraid to ask what kind of revenge."

"You should be," she answered, then paused. "I changed numbers on Lions Imports audited financial statements." She tossed the statements in her lap onto the coffee table. "I then signed the firm's name on the report, in Craig's handwriting. Next, I sent the whole package to Revenue Canada. One day, a man named Kelly Faust from Special Investigations called, not to investigate the statement's numbers, but to blackmail me into helping him cover up the Ice Craft fraud. Unfortunately, things got out of control . . . people died." Isobel gazed at the statements.

Jillian started to rock back and forth. She wondered if Alex had reached Revenue Canada yet. "Do you know who killed Marlena?"

She gazed at the fish tank. "Kelly and I followed her out of the casino. We saw her enter a suite." She hesitated. "He told me to wait for him in our room because he wanted to talk to her for a minute. That's all I know."

She looked at Jillian. "I saw him attack you on the pier. I was hoping you'd drown him."

Jillian rubbed hot, clammy hands on her pant leg. "How come I didn't see you there?"

"I was in disguise." Isobel shook her head. "Ridiculous, isn't it, but when you're being manipulated by unbalanced people, the consequences usually are ridiculous."

She slipped her hand into her purse. "With maturer, more secure men, things would have worked out, but people in three-piece suits don't hold a monopoly on stability."

Jillian folded her arms to keep from shaking. She was afraid to ask the next question, but she had to know.

"You didn't, by any chance, try to open a certain cubicle in the casino's washroom, did you?"

Isobel's eyes became glassy. She looked away. "Kelly demanded that I bring you to him. He thought he could get Alex's cooperation if you were with us. But then Marlena showed up and, despite the wig I had on, she recognized me right away."

"Is that when you followed her out of the casino?"

She slowly nodded.

"Oh, Isobel."

"When I left Kelly to come up here, he said that if I wanted to stay alive, no one could know that I was in this apartment." A tear rolled down Isobel's cheek as a revolver emerged from her purse. "He's parked in front of the building, you see; waiting for me in the car. . . . He must have seen you come up."

Jillian's face turned crimson. Her legs tingled. She

couldn't stand up. "No, Isobel! Please put the gun away!"

"He will kill me," she insisted, "if I don't do this."

The telephone rang. Both women looked at it, then at one another.

Isobel quickly wiped her eyes. "I'm sorry."

"No!"

The gun shook. Jillian stared at the stainless steel barrel and couldn't breathe.

"Isobel, please! Wait!"

She scrambled down the sofa — the gun fired. The clown barbs and black mollies darted around the fish tank as she fell, and when Isobel saw the blood, she ran.

TWENTY-EIGHT

Fifteen minutes after closing time, Alex crept out of a bathroom on his floor at Revenue Canada and headed for the stairwell. With his picture I.D. hanging from his neck, he'd had no trouble passing both security guards at the elevators in the lobby. Evidently, Revenue Canada hadn't banned him from the building, but he hadn't wanted to be seen by the staff either, which was why he'd left the elevator and, adopting Jillian's tactic, sought refuge in the bathroom.

In the stairwell, the door to the floor above him opened, and two people he recognized from other departments hurried down the steps. They smiled at Alex as they passed him. He nodded and hurried on. The stairwell doors were supposed to be locked, as security restrictions prevented staff members from visiting departments on other floors without authorization. Once in a while, Alex's supervisor had given him permission to deliver documents to employees in other areas of the building. A couple of times, he'd even been given keys to stairwell doors, which he'd had copied. Alex liked to collect keys; had never much cared for locked doors of any kind.

The floor where Special Investigations was located looked abandoned. Alex walked cautiously between the desks and partitions. He listened for bits of conversation, rattling papers, a pushed chair, but the area was silent.

He found Kelly Faust's name on a door and knocked

softly. There was no answer. He tried the handle but the door was locked. Someone walked up behind him. Turning around, Alex saw a tall pudgy man carrying a worn briefcase.

Darius Ridgegold stared at his I.D. "I haven't seen you before."

"I'm fairly new here." He shook Ridgegold's hand. "I'm supposed to see Kelly Faust."

"Who's your supervisor?"

"Mitchell Koehler. Would it be okay to wait in Mr. Faust's office?"

"Since he's opened mine enough times." Ridgegold removed a key from his pocket. "Don't tell him I let you in, all right?"

"Sure." Alex stepped inside, sat down at Faust's desk and called Jillian.

While the phone rang, he gazed at a photograph of an obese, middle-aged man. He rummaged through the drawers of Faust's desk until he reached a locked one on the bottom left hand side. He hung up the phone, then grabbing a letter opener, tried to pry the drawer open.

An object dropped onto the desk. Alex looked up and saw a man in his early forties point to the key that lay before him. His eye was bruised and there was a cut above it. His expression was solemn, tired.

"Go ahead," Faust said, "use it."

Cautiously, Alex unlocked the drawer. He found his and Andy's personnel records in the top two folders. Alex stared at Faust, then emptied the drawer. Among the papers was an address book, plus several pornographic photographs of Alfred Lin and Marlena Margolin. Again, Alex looked at Faust, then skimmed over bank books and letters while Faust explained a rather elaborate blackmail scheme intended to discredit certain Revenue Canada personnel.

"Why did you kill Andy?"

"I had no choice. He caught me in his bedroom after you left." Faust adjusted his father's glasses. "I had to know what you'd discovered at Ice Craft."

"Which is why you tried to grab the files from me in the parking lot."

"Obviously."

"Since you were *obviously* carrying a razor blade at the time, I think you intended to do more than steal files." Alex glared at him. "Did you wear your ski mask for Andy too, or was he allowed to see his killer?"

"I usually wore the mask, but it interfered with my glasses, so I used it only when necessary. Your dramatic display on the pier last night forced me to resort to larger and noisier weapons than razor blades."

As Faust slipped his hand into his pocket, Alex threw the photograph at him. Grabbing the files, he raced out the door and headed for the stairwell. As he ran, he tucked the files under his left arm, and was reaching for his own weapon when a shot rang out.

Faust was running towards him when Alex raised his pistol to return the fire. The elevator doors opened and a cleaning woman pushed a cart onto the floor. She saw Alex, then the gun. She looked at Faust whose weapon had vanished. The woman abandoned the cart, and retreated back into the elevator. She stepped to one side, out of view, and began hitting the "close" button repeatedly.

Alex disappeared into the stairwell and started down the steps. At the landing below, he heard voices on the other side of the door. Halfway to the next floor, footsteps hurried down the steps behind him.

Alex turned around and found himself facing the blue steel barrel of Faust's revolver. Faust stood on the landing above him. Holding the gun with both hands, he moved down one step, then another.

"I've been following you since the island," he panted, and paused to catch his breath, "and I'm not ready to part quite yet."

Alex gripped his own weapon. "Was Barker involved

with the plan to kill us on the island?"

"I've never met Mr. Barker."

"You were blackmailing him and Sam Roche, weren't you?"

"Roche was more accessible, but now that I've finally learned all about Barker's many activities, he could be of use in the future."

"How did you hear about the fraud in the first place?"

"After I received an intriguing letter from Craig McBride at Silby & Morrow, I put Barker's controller on my payroll. McBride claimed that Isobel Cameron had falsified Lions Imports financial statements, and that Barker apparently liked the changes, since it put him in a better tax position. Several weeks later, the controller told me about some unusual transactions with Roche. I contacted Roche and offered to keep the income tax authorities off his back, for a price. He was worried about Silby & Morrow finding out. Since McBride's claim was true, I was able to volunteer Ms. Cameron's help and cooperation."

Alex glared at him. "You're a resourceful guy."

Each man measured the distance and angle from the other; tried to determine the probability of firing without being hit in return.

"You enjoy killing people, don't you?" Alex stated.

"Nonsense. I will admit, though, that breaking the law is far more interesting than obeying it. I can understand why Barker does it so freely." A faint smile crossed Kelly's lips. "I've succeeded because businessmen aren't so much dangerous as frightened and corrupt. I exploit them, you see. They deserve it. Of course, my friend in the blue Oldsmobile is one of those rare breeds who's both dangerous and frightened."

"What's his role in the fraud?"

"None. The man just owed me a favour, that's all."

Alex shook his head. "Will you kill Isobel Cameron, too?"

Kelly stared at him. "She could become quite accident-prone. Also, with her career about to disintegrate, suicide's a viable option."

"Why didn't you use a razor blade on Sam Roche?"

"Given his history and the kind of party he was hosting that night, it seemed more believable to have him die of a drug overdose."

"How believable was Marlena Margolin's alleged suicide?"

"That was an impulsive act. Besides, it was the only means available."

"Why kill her?"

"Two hours after Roche died, I approached Marlena with the photographs you saw in my desk drawer."

"How did you get the pictures?"

"From Roche's bedroom. Regrettably, Mrs. Margolin wasn't interested in paying to have them returned. When she spotted me in the casino yesterday, I knew I had to stop the lady before she and Barker made life difficult."

"Were you on the island to see her?"

"To find out what the place was about, like everyone else, it seemed. I didn't know Mrs. Margolin would be there."

From the stairs above, a woman said, "You shouldn't have gone to that island, Kelly."

Footsteps drew closer until Alex saw a shaken and angry-looking blonde. She stood three steps from the landing above, and peered down at him.

Alex glanced at the short, stainless steel barrel of her Colt revolver.

"How did you get in?" Kelly stepped up to the landing. "In fact, how did you get here?"

"When I discovered that you'd left without me, I walked until I managed to hail a cab. With all the people coming and going at closing time, it was easy to get by the guards." Isobel kept her eyes on Faust. "I was already on the floor when you started chasing Alex. After the cleaning lady's appearance, I decided that Alex needed help."

"Considering your role in all of this," Kelly remarked, "helping Alex is a rather strange position to take."

"There's been far too many deaths; too many lives destroyed." She looked at Alex, then quickly turned to Kelly. "I wish I'd had the courage to stop you ages ago, but since you think that suicide's a viable option for me, it's time we ended this nightmarish relationship."

"Are you sure?" Kelly pointed his revolver at Alex's face. "Maybe you should think about creating a new business partnership with me. I'll give you a hundred thousand dollars, just to show how serious I am about the offer." He gazed at her. "I could have the cash in an hour."

Her smile was merciless. "Why don't you take another razor blade, place it against your throat, and slice deeply?"

"I'm afraid I'm not the suicidal type."

"If I were you, I wouldn't keep the gun pointed at Alex too long. Somehow, I don't think he'd mind if I shot you."

Alex studied her. "You were on the island, weren't you?"

She nodded. "At first, I thought Kelly had left without me, but no such luck. Then I had to endure the humiliation of hiding in the back seat while he played cat and mouse with you and Jillian."

"As we followed you back to Vancouver," Kelly said, "Isobel remembered spotting Tristan Wells at Silby & Morrow the night I visited her there. She said Tristan never stayed late as a rule, yet he was suddenly around a great deal."

Alex squeezed the files under his arm.

"This morning, Isobel made sure Tristan was at work. She also managed to remove a set of personal keys from the jacket he apparently hates to wear indoors. After her lunch with Les Silby, I picked her up at two-thirty, a block from the restaurant, as we'd arranged. She then called her office to make sure Tristan was still there. After that, we drove to his apartment to confirm her suspicions. While Isobel searched his place I waited in the car." He started to smile. "You can imagine my surprise when I saw you drop off Miss Scott." He turned to Isobel. "I'm sorry I didn't wait for you, but I had to find out where Alex was going."

"It didn't matter. When Jillian told me where Alex was heading, I knew you wouldn't be far behind."

Kelly's eyes grew narrow and cold. "I assume you shot the girl?"

While Isobel glowered at him, sweat emerged on Alex's temples. His heart pumped faster. "You didn't, did you?"

Her face grew pale. "He said he'd kill me if I let anyone see me there."

"Oh, God."

"I think the bullet hit her upper arm. I . . . I'm sure she'll survive. After I left the building, I found a public phone and called 911." Isobel cocked the hammer on her revolver. "I'm so sorry."

"You can't win with me, Alex." Kelly spoke softly. "My father always said I was beyond redemption. Most people are beyond redemption."

Alex began to run down the stairs.

"Alex!" Kelly aimed at him.

Isobel fired her weapon, hitting Kelly in the shoulder while his own gun went off, missing Alex completely. Kelly fell as he fired again. This time, he didn't miss.

The files fell as Alex grabbed his left side and collapsed onto the landing. He pulled himself to his knees, then straightened up. As Kelly got up and aimed at Isobel, Alex shot him in the thigh. Alex staggered to his feet, started down the next set of steps and fell again. Seconds later, a stairwell door flew open and two cops appeared with their weapons pointed at him.

"There's a girl!" he shouted. "She's been shot!"

The cops glanced at one another as Alex's blood trickled down the steps.

TWENTY-NINE

Jillian adjusted the sling around her left arm. She'd been found by the building manager, who'd received an anxious phone call about gunshots from the tenant next door. While she was receiving treatment at the St. Paul's Hospital emergency room, Alex and Kelly Faust were wheeled in on gurneys. The bullet from Faust's gun had torn a strip of flesh from Alex's side. Hours later, after their discharge and subsequent statements to the police, Alex had brought her back here to collect her things.

As he helped her pack her clothes in a shopping bag, he repeated his conversation with Faust. He told her everything up to the shootings, at which point his memory became fuzzy.

"What will happen to Faust now?"

"There'll be murder and attempted murder charges, and God knows what else, once the fraud people have examined his files. There might also be some sort of psychiatric assessment."

"Sounds like he doesn't have much of a life left."

"At least he's alive, which is more than we can say for Sam and Marlena," he said, and paused, "and Andy."

Alex carried Jillian's shopping bag into the living room.

"If I hadn't assumed it was Marlena on the other side of the bathroom door in the casino, then maybe I would have had the guts to step out of the cubicle," she said. "I would have seen Isobel and talked to her; might have prevented all the violence last night."

"If I'd told you my suspicions about Isobel, you wouldn't have stayed in this apartment to talk to her."

"You didn't know she'd be here."

"And you couldn't have known that Marlena was a target. So all this guilt stuff is pointless."

She sat on the sofa as Alex walked to the kitchen. "Want some orange juice?"

"No, thanks."

At the hospital, Jillian had begun to understand what it was about the conflicts and arguments between partners that had been bothering her. It was the strong, unaffected smile Isobel wore after every insult. Her responses had always seemed unnatural: calm and remote.

"Alex, it's almost midnight. I think I should go home."

"You can't quite yet." He strolled into the living room. "Les wants to see you. He's on his way over."

"Thanks a bunch."

A minute later, the buzzer rang and Les hesitantly entered the room. Jillian saw the shock and dismay on his face as he spotted the bloodstain on the sofa. He tried not to stare at the sling cradling her arm.

"How badly were you hurt?"

"I'm okay. Doctor said I'll be fine before I know it."

"If I'd seen Isobel at the casino, I could have stopped all this." His voice was apologetic, guilt-ridden.

"She was wearing a wig," Alex explained. "Easy for someone to spot at close range, but not halfway across the room."

"I spoke to her lawyer." Les looked at Jillian.

"Did you speak to Isobel?"

"She wouldn't see me."

"Sit down, Les." Alex offered him his chair. "Can I get you something to drink?"

"Thank you, no." He sat next to Jillian on the sofa. "Isobel has a few problems to work out."

Jillian glanced at Alex, then turned to Les. "How's Jerry?"

"Not good."

Alex placed his hand over his wound and grimaced as he sat down. "What's happened with Tony Barker?"

"The cops think he's somewhere in France," Les replied. "Apparently, his wife's been there about six months, undergoing some sort of treatment for a rare skin disease. Alfred's going to pursue every legal option he has to see that Barker repays the money he and Sam Roche took from Ice Craft."

"How will Ice Craft manage until then?" Alex asked.

"Relatives will help him out. Alfred's wife arrives from Malaysia tomorrow and everything will be fine."

Alex doubted it. Alfred's affair would probably be revealed at Faust's trial. Among the files confiscated in the stairwell were Sam Roche's pornographic photos of Alfred and Marlena: evidence that would be used to connect Faust to both Roche's and Marlena's murder.

"So," Les said, turning to Jillian, "when can you come back to work?"

"Soon, I guess."

"Good. The office is in chaos."

The door flew open and Tristan Wells barged into the room. It took two seconds for Jillian to realize this was his apartment, and that she should probably thank him for the use of the place.

"Oh, my darling idiot child, why did you stand in front of the gun?" he said. "You should have ducked!"

She looked at Alex. "Don't tell me this is your special friend."

"Okay, I won't, but he's the one who fetched your purse after you fainted in the storage room." Alex turned to Tristan. "I thought you were still staying with your parents."

"I had a hot date tonight and had to come back here for my lucky clothes."

He smiled at Les, hoping he wouldn't ask about a certain

date with a bookkeeper he was supposed to have cancelled.

"Hi, Les."

"Hello."

Tristan turned to Jillian. "I was worried about you."

"I hope my brush with death didn't spoil your evening."

"I saw an ambulance rush down the street as I drove up, but I had no idea you were in it until the manager accosted me in the hallway. I phoned the hospital and was told you'd be fine, so I thought, why waste the evening?"

Jillian rolled her eyes.

"Alex later called my cell phone number and told me what happened on Barker's island," he added. "Now that the bad guys have been caught, I can sleep in my own apartment again. I hope you guys took good care of my fish."

"I can't believe it. The office pervert turns into the office spy." Jillian turned to Alex. "You should have told me."

"I didn't think you'd believe me."

"I would have believed Les."

Everyone looked at the senior partner.

"Alex didn't trust him," Tristan stated, "and he didn't trust Alex or me, which is why I was fired this afternoon, right, Les?"

Jillian smiled at her boss. "Oh?"

"That's part of the reason," he answered, "but since you've helped the firm, in your own unusual way, and haven't yet finished articling, you can come back, if you like."

"With a raise?"

"No."

"Thank you, I accept." He took Jillian's hand and kissed it noisily. "Maybe we should have dinner one night to celebrate this happy ending."

"Tristan, I've been shot, chased, kidnapped, nearly run over, and almost drowned, but dinner with you would kill me."

"Well, think about it."

She turned to Alex. "When are you going back to work?"

"Don't know. I'm supposed to take it easy a few days. I don't even know if Revenue Canada will want me back."

"I'm sure they'll understand why you kept the files."

"Why not start your own detective agency?" Tristan suggested. "With your obsessive need to be in charge and your bizarre methods of solving problems you'll never last with Revenue Canada anyway."

"I don't want to spy on the sleazy affairs of married people."

"What about the sleazy affairs of corporations? Start an agency that specializes in white collar criminal investigations."

"Actually, I'm thinking about taking a short trip to California."

"His parents live in Palm Springs," Tristan said to Jillian. "Lucky or what?"

She turned to Alex. "I thought you said they lived in Montreal."

"They sold that hotel, then retired, more or less."

"Are your adopted parents American?"

"He's not adopted." Tristan glanced at Alex who was frantically shaking his head. "His dad's American. His mom's Canadian, though."

"Thanks a bunch," he murmured.

Jillian's green eyes blazed as her most ferocious expressions began to surface. There was silent, cynical outrage followed by offended, moralistic hurt, and Alex's personal favourite, vengeful, contemptuous disgust for his entire being.

"He has a sister living in Australia, one brother operating the family hotel in London, plus another brother and sister operating their New York hotel," Tristan said.

Jillian stared at Alex. "Did you have to lie about your family?"

"I don't blame you for being angry."

"I suppose the stuff about your grandmother was a lie

too."

"No, and she wouldn't have been thrilled with the lie about my family either." Alex stared into his glass. "I did feel like an outcast when they moved east, but my grandmother taught me about forgiveness, among other things." He looked at her. "It's an acquired skill."

Jillian rested her head against the sofa. "I hate lies."

Alex brushed his hand over the blue and white sweater Andy's mom had knitted him last month. "Have you got any plans over the next couple of days?"

"She'll be resting at home," Les stated as he turned to her. "I'll drive you there now, if you like."

Alex said, "I can take her home, Les."

"Not if you're on medication."

"She's welcome to stay the night," Tristan offered.

"Time to go." She stood up, feeling woozy and swaying slightly as a result of pain killers.

"See you at work, my love." Tristan kissed her hand. "If you get lonely during your convalescence, give me a call."

"Jillian, I need your help with one more thing," Alex said quickly.

Les started to protest but Alex cut him off.

"I'd like you to meet Andy's parents. I think they'd believe my story if you were with me. I know they'd want to meet you."

The room was silent. The only things that moved were the clown barbs and black mollies in Tristan's fish tank.

"I suppose we could talk about how strange you are." She picked up her shopping bag.

"They'd like that."

Les took the bag from her and turned to Tristan. "Be on time tomorrow."

"Don't worry, I won't let you down. I know we can make it work this time."

Jillian gave Les a hopeless, now-see-what-you've-done look, then followed him out the door.